THE TIMEKEEPER'S QUEST

BY MUVHANGO MAHOOA

Copyright © 2024 by Muvhango Mahooa.

The right of Muvhango mahooa to be identified as the author of the work has been asserted by him in accordance to the copyright. Design and patents Act of 1988.

ALL RIGHTS RESERVED. No part of this publication may be reproduced, stored in a retrieval system, or transmitted in any form of by any means, electronic, mechanical, photocopying, recording or otherwise, without the prior permission of the publishers, except for the use of brief quotations in a book review.

This is a work of fiction. Names, characters, places and incidents are a product of the authors imagination or are used fictitiously. Any resemblance to actual persons, living or dead, business establishments, events or locales is entirely coincidental.

Cover & artwork designed with CANVA by Muvhango mahooa.

Muvhangomahooa17@gmail.com

"Time is a canvas, painted with moments of joy, sorrow, and wonder. Every second is a brushstroke, crafting a masterpiece of memory and experience."

-MUVHANGO MAHOOA

Table of contents

Prologue : The time stream's warning.
Chapter 1 : The wilting bouquet.
Chapter 2 : The forgotten library.
Chapter 3 : The mysterious stranger.
Chapter 4 : The secret garden.
Chapter 5 : The afterlife.
Chapter 6 : The quantum prophecy.
Chapter 7 : The quantum warrior.
Chapter 8 : The quantum prophecy unveiled.
Chapter 9 : The hidden lab.
Chapter 10 : The crystal temple.
Chapter 11 : The next leap.
Chapter 12 : The pathway through the multiverse.
Chapter 13 : The trials.
Chapter 14 : The lost city.
Chapter 15 : The unveiling.
Chapter 16 : The guardian of the multiverse.
Chapter 17 : The time traveller's dilemma.
Chapter 18 : The temple of Ptah.
Chapter 19 : The guardian of time.
Chapter 20 : The truth revealed.
Chapter 21 : The final battle.
Chapter 22: The final confrontation.

Epilogue : Emilia's legacy.

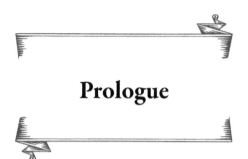

Prologue

In the depths of the time stream, a disturbance echoed through the ages. A rogue temporal entity, known only as The Time Reaver, threatened to unravel the very fabric of time itself.

The Guardian, a mysterious figure sworn to protect the time stream, sensed the disturbance and knew that action was necessary. She reached out across the ages, seeking a champion to wield the power of the Timekeeper's Armour and defend the time stream against The Time Reaver's evil plans.

In a small village on a distant planet, a young woman named Emilia felt an inexplicable call to adventure. She was unaware of the time stream's danger, but her destiny was about to become intertwined with the fate of the universe.

The Guardian's whisper echoed in Emilia's mind: "The time stream needs you, Emilia. Will you answer the call?"

And so, Emilia's journey began, a journey that would take her across time and space, testing her courage and wits against the forces of darkness.

Chapter 1

Emilia's eyes wandered across the withering petals, her heart aching as she gazed upon the once-vibrant flower farm. The familiar scent of blooming roses and fresh earth now mingled with the sweet hint of decay. She stepped out of the car and onto the gravel driveway, the crunching sound beneath her feet echoing through the stillness.

As she approached the farmhouse, memories flooded her mind. Childhood summers spent playing among the rows of sunflowers, her mother's warm smile as they tended to the gardens together, and the countless bouquets her father carefully crafted for special occasions. The farm had always been a sanctuary, a place where love and beauty flourished. But now, the fading petals seemed to whisper a different story.

Emilia's thoughts drifted to the letter that had brought her back to the farm. Her father's words, laced with a mix of desperation and hope, had stirred a sense of responsibility within her. She had to come home, to face the struggles head-on and find a way to revive the farm.

As she entered the farmhouse, the creaking floorboards beneath her feet seemed to groan in protest. The once-warm interior now felt chilly and neglected. Emilia's gaze fell upon the old family photographs adorning the walls, their smiles and laughter a stark contrast to the sombre atmosphere.

"Emilia, is that you?" her father called from the kitchen, his voice weary but welcoming.

"It's me, Dad," she replied, her voice softening as she entered the kitchen.

Her father, once robust and full of life, now appeared frail and worn. The lines on his face seemed deeper, etched by worry and hard work. Emilia's heart swelled with compassion as she embraced him tightly.

"I'm so glad you're home, kiddo," he whispered, his voice cracking with emotion.

As they pulled back, Emilia noticed the stack of unopened bills and letters on the kitchen table, the words "Overdue" and "Final Notice" jumping out at her. Her father's eyes met hers, and he nodded solemnly.

"We've been struggling, Emilia. The disease affecting the flowers... it's like nothing I've ever seen before. I've tried every remedy, every pesticide, but nothing seems to work."

Emilia's mind raced with questions and concerns, but she knew this wasn't the time for solutions. She needed to understand the full extent of the problem, to see the farm's condition with her own eyes.

"Show me," she said, her voice firm but gentle.

Her father nodded, and together they stepped out into the wilting world of the flower farm. As they walked, Emilia's heart ached with every step, the fading petals whispering a haunting melody of loss and longing.

As they walked through the farm, Emilia's father pointed out the various sections, each once bursting with life and colour. Now, the petals hung limp and wilted, like the hopes and dreams of the family.

"The roses were always your mother's favourite," James said, his voice cracking as he gazed upon the barren bushes. "She'd spend hours tending to them, coaxing them to bloom."

Emilia's heart ached as she remembered her mother's gentle touch and the way the roses seemed to respond to her love. She reached out and gently touched a wilted petal, feeling the softness and fragility of life.

"What happened, Dad?" Emilia asked, her voice barely above a whisper. "What's causing this disease?"

James sighed, his shoulders slumping under the weight of defeat. "We don't know, kiddo. We've tried every remedy, every pesticide, but nothing seems to work. It's like the flowers are just giving up."

Emilia's mind raced with questions and concerns. She knew that her father had always been a proud man, dedicated to the farm and their family's legacy. Seeing him so defeated and helpless broke her heart.

As they approached the old greenhouse, Emilia noticed a strange symbol etched into the door. It looked like a cross between a scientific formula and a mystical sigil.

"What's this?" Emilia asked, tracing the symbol with her finger.

James hesitated, his eyes darting around nervously. "Oh, that? Just an old experiment, kiddo. Don't mind that."

Emilia's curiosity was piqued. She knew that her father was hiding something, but she didn't press the issue. Not yet.

As they entered the greenhouse, Emilia was struck by the stark contrast between the withering flowers outside and the lush, vibrant plants within. The air was warm and humid, filled with the scent of blooming orchids and the soft hum of life.

"This is incredible," Emilia breathed, her eyes wide with wonder. "How are these plants thriving while the others are dying?"

James smiled, a hint of pride in his eyes. "This is my latest experiment, kiddo. A special soil blend and a new irrigation system. I was hoping to create a controlled environment, one that would help us understand what's killing the flowers outside."

Emilia's mind raced with possibilities. Could this greenhouse hold the key to saving the farm? And what secrets was her father hiding behind the strange symbol and his hesitant demeanour? She knew that she had to dig deeper, to uncover the truth behind the fading petals and the mysterious forces at work on the farm.

As Emilia explored the greenhouse, she noticed a series of journals and notebooks scattered among the plants. They were filled with her father's handwriting, detailing his experiments and observations.

"Dad, what's this?" Emilia asked, holding up a journal.

James hesitated, his eyes darting to the journal and back to Emilia. "Oh, just my notes, kiddo. Nothing important."

Emilia's curiosity was piqued. She began flipping through the pages, noticing strange symbols and diagrams alongside the notes.

"What's this symbol?" Emilia asked, pointing to a recurring image.

James sighed, his shoulders slumping. "That's just an old family recipe, kiddo. For the soil blend."

Emilia's eyes narrowed. She knew her father was hiding something.

As she continued reading, Emilia discovered a series of cryptic messages and codes woven throughout the journals. They seemed to point to a deeper mystery, one connected to the farm's decline.

"Dad, what's going on?" Emilia asked, her voice firm but gentle.

James looked away, his eyes avoiding hers. "I'll tell you later, kiddo. Let's focus on saving the farm first."

Emilia nodded, but her mind raced with questions. What secrets was her father keeping? And how were they connected to the fading petals?

As the sun began to set, Emilia and her father walked back to the farmhouse, the silence between them thick with unspoken questions.

Chapter 2

Emilia's mind raced with questions as she helped her father with dinner. She couldn't shake the feeling that he was hiding something important. After they finished eating, Emilia decided to explore the farmhouse, searching for answers.

She wandered into the living room, noticing a door she hadn't seen before. It was hidden behind a bookshelf, and the doorknob was covered in dust.

"Where does this lead?" Emilia asked her father, pointing to the door.

James hesitated, his eyes darting to the door and back to Emilia. "Oh, that? Just an old storage room, kiddo. Nothing important."

Emilia's curiosity was piqued. She opened the door, revealing a narrow staircase leading down into darkness.

"Dad, what's down here?" Emilia asked, her voice firm but gentle.

James sighed, his shoulders slumping. "Just an old library, kiddo. Been locked away for years."

Emilia's heart raced as she descended the stairs, her father following closely behind. The air grew thick with dust and the scent of old books.

At the bottom, Emilia found herself in a small, dimly lit room filled with shelves of ancient tomes and mysterious artefacts.

"Welcome to the forgotten library," James said, his voice barely above a whisper.

Emilia's eyes widened as she explored the shelves, running her fingers over the spines of the books.

"What secrets are hidden here?" Emilia asked, her voice full of wonder.

James smiled, his eyes twinkling in the dim light. "Ah, kiddo, that's for you to discover."

As Emilia delved deeper into the library, she noticed a section dedicated to botany and horticulture. The books were old and worn, but the illustrations of plants and flowers were incredibly detailed. She ran her fingers over the pages, feeling a connection to the natural world.

"Dad, look at this!" Emilia exclaimed, holding up a book with a beautiful illustration of a rose.

James smiled, his eyes nostalgic. "Ah, yes. Your mother used to love that book. She'd spend hours poring over it, learning about new species and techniques."

Emilia's heart swelled with love for her mother, who had passed away a few years ago. She had been a kind and gentle soul, always nurturing and caring for others.

As Emilia continued exploring, she stumbled upon a mysterious book with strange symbols and diagrams. The cover was old and worn, but the pages inside were filled with handwritten notes and illustrations.

"What's this?" Emilia asked, holding up the book.

James hesitated, his eyes darting to the book and back to Emilia. "Oh, that? Just an old journal, kiddo. Nothing important."

Emilia's curiosity was piqued. She began flipping through the pages, noticing that the symbols and diagrams seemed to match the ones she had seen in her father's journals.

"Dad, this looks like your handwriting," Emilia said, her voice firm but gentle.

THE TIME KEEPER'S QUEST

James sighed, his shoulders slumping. "Okay, kiddo. I'll tell you. That's my old research journal. I was working on a project, trying to create a new species of flower."

Emilia's eyes widened in amazement. "A new species? What kind of flower?"

James smiled, his eyes twinkling. "Ah, kiddo, that's the best part. I was trying to create a flower that would bloom forever."

Emilia's heart raced with excitement. "That's impossible!"

James chuckled. "I know it sounds crazy, but I was convinced it could be done. I spent years researching and experimenting, but I never quite got it right."

Emilia's mind raced with questions and possibilities. She couldn't believe that her father had been working on such an incredible project.

As they continued exploring the library, Emilia stumbled upon a hidden compartment in the bookshelf. Inside, she found a small, delicate box with a strange symbol etched onto its lid.

"What's this?" Emilia asked, holding up the box.

James hesitated, his eyes darting to the box and back to Emilia. "Oh, that? Just an old trinket, kiddo. Nothing important."

Emilia's curiosity was piqued. She opened the box, revealing a beautiful, glowing seed inside.

"Wow!" Emilia exclaimed. "What is this?"

James smiled, his eyes twinkling. "Ah, kiddo, that's the last piece of the puzzle. That's the forever flower seed."

Emilia's heart raced with excitement. She couldn't believe that she was holding the key to her father's life's work.

As they left the library, Emilia turned to her father with a determined look on her face.

"Dad, we're going to make this happen. We're going to create the forever flower."

James smiled, his eyes shining with pride. "I knew you'd see it, kiddo. Let's get to work."

Emilia's determination ignited a fire within her father's eyes. Together, they began pouring over the research and notes, studying the forever flower seed and its properties.

As the night wore on, Emilia's mind raced with questions and ideas. She couldn't believe the significance of the discovery and the potential impact it could have on the world.

"Dad, what if we could use this seed to create a whole garden of forever flowers?" Emilia asked, her excitement growing.

James smiled, his eyes twinkling. "That's the dream, kiddo. And I think we can do it."

As they worked, Emilia noticed strange noises coming from outside the library. At first, she thought it was just the wind or the creaks and groans of the old farmhouse, but then she heard footsteps.

"Dad, do you hear that?" Emilia asked, her voice barely above a whisper.

James paused, his head cocked to the side. "Hear what?"

Emilia frowned, her heart beating faster. "The footsteps. It sounds like someone's walking around the house."

James's expression turned serious. "That's impossible. We're in the middle of nowhere. There's no one around for miles."

Emilia's curiosity got the better of her. She quietly got up and made her way to the door, her father following closely behind.

As they approached the entrance, the footsteps grew louder. Emilia slowly turned the handle and opened the door, revealing a figure standing in the shadows.

"Who's there?" Emilia called out, her voice firm but cautious.

The figure stepped forward, revealing a young woman with piercing green eyes and long, curly brown hair.

"Hi," the woman said, her smile warm and friendly. "My name is Sophia. I've been sent to help you."

Emilia's eyes narrowed. "Sent by who?"

Sophia hesitated, her eyes darting to James and back to Emilia. "By someone who cares about your work. Someone who wants to see the forever flower bloom."

Emilia's mind raced with questions, but before she could ask any of them, Sophia vanished into thin air.

Emilia spun around, her heart racing. "What just happened?"

James's expression was grim. "I don't know, kiddo. But I think we're in for a wild ride."

Chapter 3

Emilia's mind was reeling from the sudden appearance and disappearance of Sophia. She couldn't shake off the feeling that something strange was going on.

"Dad, what just happened?" Emilia asked, her voice laced with concern.

James frowned, his eyes scanning the surrounding area. "I don't know, kiddo. But I think we should be careful. We don't know who that woman was or what she wants."

Emilia nodded in agreement. She couldn't believe how much her life had changed in just a few days. First, the mysterious disease affecting the flowers, and now a strange woman appearing out of nowhere.

As they went back inside, Emilia couldn't help but feel like they were being watched. She kept looking over her shoulder, expecting to see Sophia again.

"Dad, I think we should try to find out who Sophia is," Emilia said, her curiosity getting the better of her.

James nodded. "I agree. But we need to be careful. We don't know what we're dealing with here."

Emilia's mind was racing with questions. Who was Sophia? What did she want? And how did she vanish into thin air?

As they continued their research, Emilia couldn't shake off the feeling that Sophia was still out there, watching them.

As the days passed, Emilia and James delved deeper into their research, but the mysterious stranger, Sophia, remained a constant enigma. Emilia's fascination with Sophia's appearance and disappearance only grew stronger, and she found herself scouring the farmhouse and surrounding areas for any clues.

One afternoon, while exploring the attic, Emilia stumbled upon an old, dusty trunk with a strange symbol etched onto its lid. As she opened it, she discovered a collection of letters and photographs that seemed to belong to her mother.

Among the letters, Emilia found a cryptic message that read: "The truth lies in the petals." Emilia's heart raced as she wondered if this was a clue to unlocking the secrets of the forever flower.

As she continued to explore the trunk, Emilia found a photograph of her mother standing next to a beautiful, glowing flower. The flower seemed to radiate an otherworldly light, and Emilia felt an inexplicable connection to it.

Suddenly, Emilia heard a faint whispering in her ear. "Look closer, Emilia." It was Sophia's voice.

Emilia spun around, but Sophia was nowhere to be seen. She turned her attention back to the photograph and examined it more closely. That's when she noticed something strange - the flower in the picture seemed to be made up of tiny, glowing petals that looked eerily similar to the symbol on the trunk's lid.

Emilia's mind raced with questions. What did this symbol mean? And how was it connected to the forever flower?

As she pondered these questions, Emilia heard the whispering again. "Follow the petals, Emilia. They will lead you to the truth."

This time, Emilia decided to follow the mysterious voice. She carefully removed the photograph from the trunk and began to examine it more closely. As she did, the glowing petals began to shimmer and shine, revealing a hidden message that read: "Meet me at the old oak tree at midnight."

Emilia's heart raced with excitement and a hint of fear. What would she find at the old oak tree? And who was behind the mysterious messages?

As midnight approached, Emilia made her way to the old oak tree, her heart pounding with anticipation. The moon cast eerie shadows on the ground, and the wind rustled through the leaves, creating an unsettling atmosphere.

Suddenly, a figure emerged from the darkness. It was Sophia, her eyes gleaming with an otherworldly intensity.

"Follow me," Sophia whispered, beckoning Emilia to follow her.

Emilia hesitated, her instincts screaming warning signals. But her curiosity got the better of her, and she trailed Sophia through the winding paths of the forest.

They arrived at a clearing, and Emilia gasped in wonder. In the centre of the clearing stood an enormous flower, its petals shimmering with an ethereal light.

"The forever flower," Sophia breathed, her voice full of reverence.

Emilia approached the flower, feeling an inexplicable connection to it. As she touched the petals, she felt a surge of energy course through her body.

"This is it," Sophia whispered. "This is the key to unlocking the secrets of the forever flower."

Emilia's mind reeled as she gazed at the flower in awe. She knew that her life would never be the same again.

But as she turned to Sophia, she saw something that made her blood run cold. Sophia's eyes had turned black as coal, and her smile was twisted into a malevolent grin.

"You shouldn't have come here," Sophia hissed, her voice dripping with malice.

Emilia tried to run, but her feet were rooted to the spot. Sophia raised her hand, and Emilia felt a strange energy wash over her.

As the world went dark, Emilia realized that she had made a terrible mistake. She had trusted the wrong person, and now she was paying the price.

Emilia's vision blurred, and she felt herself being pulled into a dark vortex. She tried to scream, but her voice was muffled by some unseen force. The last thing she remembered was Sophia's twisted grin before everything went black.

When Emilia came to, she found herself in a strange, dimly lit room. The walls were adorned with strange symbols, and the air was thick with the scent of incense. She tried to sit up, but a sharp pain shot through her head, making her recoil.

"Welcome, Emilia," a low, gravelly voice said from the shadows. "I see you're awake."

Emilia's eyes adjusted to the darkness, and she saw a figure cloaked in shadows. "Who are you?" she demanded, trying to keep her voice steady.

The figure stepped forward, revealing a tall, gaunt man with sunken eyes. "I am the one who has been guiding Sophia," he said, his voice dripping with malice. "And you, Emilia, are the key to unlocking the secrets of the forever flower."

Emilia's mind raced as she tried to piece together the events of the previous night. "What do you want from me?" she asked, trying to keep her fear in check.

The gaunt man smiled, revealing crooked teeth. "Oh, Emilia. I want everything. Your knowledge, your skills, your very soul."

Emilia knew she had to escape, but her body felt heavy, as if weighed down by some unseen force. She tried to struggle, but her limbs felt like lead.

The gaunt man began to chant in a language Emilia didn't understand, and the air in the room began to thicken. Emilia felt herself being pulled into a dark, abyssal void, and she knew she was running out of time.

Chapter 4

Emilia's mind raced as she tried to comprehend the gaunt man's sinister plans. She knew she had to escape, but her body felt heavy, as if weighed down by an unseen force.

Just as the gaunt man's chanting reached a fever pitch, Emilia heard a faint rustling sound coming from outside the room. The gaunt man's eyes flickered towards the door, and for a moment, his concentration wavered.

That was all the time Emilia needed. With a surge of adrenaline, she broke free from the strange force holding her down and made a run for the door.

She flung it open and found herself in a long, dark corridor. The rustling sound grew louder, and Emilia followed it to a door hidden behind a tattered curtain.

She pushed the door open and found herself in a beautiful, neglected garden. The moon was full overhead, casting an ethereal glow over the overgrown flowers and vines.

Emilia wandered through the garden, her heart pounding with excitement. She had never seen anything so beautiful in her life.

As she explored, she stumbled upon a hidden path she hadn't noticed before. It led her to a small, secret garden within the larger one.

In the centre of the secret garden stood an enormous tree, its branches twisted and gnarled with age. Emilia felt drawn to the tree, as if it held secrets she was desperate to uncover.

As she reached out to touch the trunk, a figure stepped out from behind the tree. It was Sophia, her eyes gleaming with a mischievous light.

"Welcome to my garden," Sophia said, her voice barely above a whisper. "Here, secrets bloom like flowers."

Emilia's mind reeled as she tried to understand Sophia's enigmatic words. What secrets was Sophia hiding? And what did they have to do with the forever flower?

Sophia's gaze seemed to bore into Emilia's soul, as if searching for something hidden deep within. Emilia felt a shiver run down her spine, but she stood her ground, determined to uncover the truth.

"What secrets?" Emilia asked, her voice firm but curious.

Sophia's smile grew wider, her eyes glinting with mischief. "Ah, my dear, the secrets of the forever flower are not for the faint of heart."

Emilia's frustration grew, but she knew she had to keep Sophia talking. "What do you mean?" she pressed on.

Sophia's laughter echoed through the garden, sending shivers down Emilia's spine. "The forever flower holds the key to eternal life," Sophia whispered, her voice barely audible.

Emilia's mind raced as she tried to comprehend the enormity of Sophia's words. Eternal life? Was that even possible?

As she pondered, Sophia reached out and plucked a small, delicate flower from the garden. "This is the forever flower," Sophia said, her eyes gleaming with intensity. "And with it, you can unlock the secrets of eternal life."

Emilia's heart pounded as she gazed at the flower in awe. She knew she had to have it, no matter the cost.

But as she reached out to take the flower, Sophia's hand closed around it, her grip tight. "Not so fast," Sophia said, her eyes glinting with a warning. "The forever flower comes with a price, Emilia. Are you willing to pay it?"

Emilia hesitated, her mind racing with doubts. But her desire for the flower's secrets overrode her fears. "Yes," she said finally, her voice firm. "I'll pay the price."

Sophia's smile grew wider, her eyes gleaming with triumph. "Then let us begin," she said, her voice dripping with malice.

And with that, Emilia knew she had sealed her fate. But what lay ahead, she had no idea. The mystery deepens!

Sophia's eyes seemed to gleam with a sinister light as she led Emilia deeper into the garden. They walked in silence, the only sound being the soft rustling of leaves beneath their feet.

As they turned a corner, Emilia noticed a strange symbol etched into the trunk of a nearby tree. It looked like a cross between a hieroglyph and a mathematical equation.

"What's that?" Emilia asked, her curiosity getting the better of her.

Sophia's smile grew wider. "That, my dear, is the mark of the forever flower. It's a sign that we're getting close."

Emilia's heart raced with excitement. She could feel the energy of the garden building up inside her, like a storm about to break.

As they walked further, the symbols became more frequent, until they were surrounded by a maze of strange markings.

"This is it," Sophia said, her voice barely above a whisper. "The heart of the garden. Here, the forever flower blooms."

Emilia's eyes widened as she saw a glowing light in the distance. It was the most beautiful thing she had ever seen.

But as they approached, Emilia felt a strange sensation, like her molecules were being rearranged. She looked down and saw that her hands were glowing with a soft, ethereal light.

"What's happening to me?" Emilia asked, her voice shaking with fear.

Sophia's laughter echoed through the garden, sending shivers down Emilia's spine. "You're being transformed," Sophia said, her eyes gleaming with triumph. "You're becoming one of us."

Emilia's mind raced as she tried to comprehend what was happening. She was being changed, altered in some fundamental way.

And then, everything went white.

Emilia's vision slowly returned, and she found herself in a vast, cavernous space. The air was thick with an otherworldly energy, and the walls seemed to vibrate with an eerie hum.

Sophia stood before her, eyes aglow with an unnatural light. "You have been chosen," Sophia declared, her voice dripping with reverence. "Chosen to join the ranks of the eternal ones."

Emilia's mind reeled as she struggled to comprehend the implications. Eternal ones? What did that even mean?

As she looked around, Emilia saw figures shrouded in shadows, their eyes glowing with an ethereal light. They seemed to be watching her, waiting for her to join their ranks.

Sophia reached out and took Emilia's hand, leading her deeper into the cavern. "Come," Sophia said, her voice low and hypnotic. "Let us begin your transformation."

Emilia felt a surge of fear mixed with excitement. She knew that she was stepping into the unknown, but she couldn't resist the allure of the eternal ones.

As they walked, the cavern grew darker, the air thickening with an eerie, pulsating energy. Emilia's heart raced with anticipation, her senses heightened to the point of overload.

And then, they reached the heart of the cavern. A glowing portal pulsed with an otherworldly power, beckoning Emilia to step forward.

"Welcome to eternity," Sophia whispered, her eyes aglow with an unnatural light.

Emilia hesitated, her mind racing with doubts. But Sophia's grip was firm, pulling her closer to the portal.

As Emilia stepped forward, the world around her dissolved into chaos. Colours swirled, sounds merged, and time itself seemed to warp and bend.

Emilia's consciousness expanded, her senses exploding with new perceptions. She saw the universe in a new light, the secrets of eternity unfolding before her like a tapestry.

And when the chaos subsided, Emilia found herself transformed, her very essence altered by the power of the eternal ones.

Chapter 5

Emilia's eyes adjusted slowly to the bright light that surrounded her. She found herself in a vast, open plain, with no signs of life anywhere. The sky above was a deep shade of purple, and the air was crisp and clean.

As she looked around, Emilia noticed a figure walking towards her from the distance. It was Sophia, her eyes shining with an otherworldly light.

"Welcome to the afterlife," Sophia said, her voice low and mysterious. "Here, you will find the secrets of the universe."

Emilia's mind raced with questions, but before she could ask any of them, Sophia continued.

"The afterlife is not what you think it is," Sophia said. "It's not a place of judgment or reward. It's a place of transformation."

Emilia's curiosity was piqued. "Transformation?" she repeated.

Sophia nodded. "Yes. Here, you will be transformed into a being of pure energy. You will become one with the universe."

Emilia's mind reeled as she tried to comprehend the implications. Become one with the universe? What did that even mean?

As she looked around, Emilia saw strange creatures moving in the distance. They seemed to be made of pure light, and they moved with an ethereal grace.

"What are those creatures?" Emilia asked, her voice barely above a whisper.

Sophia smiled. "Those are the guardians of the afterlife," she said. "They will guide you on your journey."

Emilia's heart raced with excitement. She knew that she was about to embark on a journey that would change her life forever.

And with that, Sophia reached out and took Emilia's hand, leading her towards the creatures of light.

As they walked, the creatures of light drew closer, their forms shifting and morphing into intricate patterns. Emilia felt a sense of wonder and trepidation, unsure of what to expect.

Sophia led her to a great crystal portal, its facets glinting in the purple light. "This is the gateway to the next realm," Sophia said, her voice filled with excitement.

Emilia hesitated, feeling a sense of awe and fear. "What lies beyond?" she asked, her voice barely above a whisper.

Sophia's smile grew wider. "The secrets of the universe," she said. "Are you ready to embrace them?"

Emilia took a deep breath and nodded. Sophia placed her hand on the crystal portal, and it began to glow with an intense light.

As they stepped through the portal, Emilia felt a sensation unlike anything she had ever experienced. Her molecules seemed to dissolve and reassemble, her consciousness expanding to encompass new dimensions.

On the other side of the portal, Emilia found herself in a realm beyond her wildest dreams. Stars and galaxies whirled around her, their light and sound filling her being.

Sophia took her hand, leading her deeper into the realm. "This is the cosmos," Sophia said, her voice filled with wonder. "Here, you will find the secrets of creation."

Emilia's mind reeled as she tried to comprehend the sheer scale and beauty of the cosmos. She knew that she had only just begun her journey, and that the secrets of the universe lay waiting for her.

As they journeyed through the cosmos, Emilia encountered strange and wondrous sights. She saw nebulae that shimmered like rainbow-colored mist, and stars that pulsed with a rhythmic intensity. She even caught a glimpse of a black hole, its event horizon warping space-time in a mesmerizing dance.

Sophia led her to a planet that seemed to be made entirely of crystal. The surface glittered like a million diamonds, refracting light into a kaleidoscope of colours.

"This is the planet of the ancients," Sophia said, her voice filled with reverence. "Here, you will find the secrets of the universe's creation."

Emilia's heart raced with excitement as she explored the planet's surface. She discovered ancient artefacts that hummed with a mysterious energy, and ruins that seemed to hold the secrets of the cosmos.

As she delved deeper into the planet's mysteries, Emilia began to uncover a hidden truth. The universe was not what it seemed, and the secrets of creation were far more complex than she had ever imagined.

Sophia's guidance led her to a hidden chamber deep within the planet's core. Inside, Emilia found an ancient artefact that pulsed with an otherworldly energy.

"This is the key to unlocking the universe's secrets," Sophia said, her eyes shining with excitement. "Are you ready to embrace the truth?"

Emilia's heart pounded with anticipation. She knew that she was on the verge of a ground-breaking discovery, one that would change her understanding of the universe forever.

As Emilia reached out to touch the artefact, she felt a sudden surge of energy course through her body. The room began to spin, and she felt herself being lifted off the ground.

Sophia's voice echoed in her mind, "Emilia, you are being chosen to fulfil an important destiny. Are you ready to accept the challenge?"

Emilia's vision blurred, and she saw a glimpse of a distant future. She saw herself standing on a hill, overlooking a vast expanse of stars. She saw a figure beside her, a being of pure light.

"Who is it?" Emilia asked, her voice barely above a whisper.

"That is your future self," Sophia replied. "You have the power to shape the course of the universe. Will you accept the challenge?"

Emilia's heart raced with excitement. She knew that she was being called to something greater than herself. She nodded her head, and the vision faded.

As the room stopped spinning, Emilia found herself back in the chamber, the artefact still pulsing with energy. Sophia smiled, her eyes shining with approval.

"Then let us begin," Sophia said. "We have much work to do."

And with that, Emilia's journey as a guardian of the universe began. She knew that she would face challenges and obstacles along the way, but she was ready to embrace her destiny.

Sophia led Emilia to a vast, circular platform that seemed to hover in mid-air. The platform was covered in intricate carvings, pulsing with a soft, blue light.

"This is the Celestial Map," Sophia said, her voice filled with reverence. "It holds the secrets of the universe's evolution."

Emilia's eyes widened as she approached the platform. She saw strange symbols etched into the surface, each one glowing with a soft, ethereal light.

Sophia placed her hand on Emilia's shoulder, guiding her closer to the platform. "Read the map, Emilia," Sophia said. "Unlock the secrets of the universe."

Emilia reached out a trembling hand, touching the platform's surface. As she did, the symbols began to glow brighter, filling her mind with visions of distant worlds and ancient civilizations.

She saw the birth of stars and galaxies, the dance of planets and moons. She saw the rise and fall of empires, the evolution of life in all its forms.

The visions faded, leaving Emilia breathless and awestruck. She turned to Sophia, her eyes shining with wonder.

"I saw everything," Emilia said, her voice barely above a whisper. "The universe's entire history."

Sophia smiled, her eyes shining with pride. "You have unlocked the secrets of the Celestial Map," Sophia said. "Now, you must use that knowledge to shape the universe's future."

Emilia's heart raced with excitement. She knew that she had been given a great responsibility, one that would change her life forever.

Chapter 6

Emilia's mind was reeling from the revelations of the Celestial Map. She had unlocked the secrets of the universe's evolution, but she knew that there was more to discover.

Sophia led her to a hidden chamber deep within the planet's core. The room was filled with strange, glowing orbs that seemed to pulse with an otherworldly energy.

"This is the Quantum Chamber," Sophia said, her voice filled with excitement. "Here, you will discover the prophecy of the quantum realm."

Emilia approached the orbs, feeling their energy coursing through her veins. Suddenly, she was enveloped in a vision of swirling colours and patterns.

She saw a glimpse of a distant future, where humanity had colonized other planets and formed a galactic government. But she also saw a darkness spreading across the galaxy, threatening to destroy entire civilizations.

Emilia's heart raced as she realized the gravity of the prophecy. She knew that she had to act quickly to prevent the impending disaster.

Sophia's voice echoed in her mind, "Emilia, you are the chosen one. You must use your knowledge to shape the future and prevent the destruction of the galaxy."

THE TIME KEEPER'S QUEST

Emilia's determination grew. She knew that she would face challenges and obstacles along the way, but she was ready to embrace her destiny.

And so, Emilia's journey as a quantum prophet began. She set out to explore the galaxy, using her knowledge to guide her and shape the future.

Emilia's first stop was the planet of Xanthea, a world renowned for its advanced technology and quantum research. She hoped to find answers to the prophecy and gather allies for her mission.

As she arrived on Xanthea, Emilia was struck by the planet's breath-taking beauty. Towering spires of crystal pierced the sky, and the air was filled with a kaleidoscope of colours.

She made her way to the planet's central research facility, where she met with the brilliant scientist, Dr. Lyra Erso.

Dr. Erso was a renowned expert in quantum physics and had dedicated her life to studying the mysteries of the universe.

"Emilia, I've been expecting you," Dr. Erso said, her eyes shining with warmth. "I've heard about your encounter with the Celestial Map. You have a crucial role to play in the future of the galaxy."

Emilia's heart raced as she shared her vision with Dr. Erso. The scientist listened intently, her expression growing increasingly serious.

"The prophecy you speak of is indeed a dire warning," Dr. Erso said. "But I believe we can prevent the catastrophe. Together, we can harness the power of quantum energy to create a new future for the galaxy."

Emilia's hope grew as she realized she had found a valuable ally in Dr. Erso. Together, they set out to gather a team of experts and embark on a quest to shape the future of the galaxy.

As Emilia and Dr. Erso delved deeper into their research, they began to unravel the mysteries of the quantum realm. They spent countless hours poring over ancient texts, seeking out forgotten knowledge and experimenting with innovative technologies.

Their breakthrough came when they discovered an ancient artefact hidden deep within the planet's core. The artefact, a glowing crystal orb, pulsed with an otherworldly energy that seemed to hold the secrets of the universe.

Dr. Erso's eyes widened as she examined the orb. "This is it, Emilia. This is the key to unlocking the power of quantum energy."

Emilia's heart raced as she reached out to touch the orb. As soon as she did, she was flooded with visions of distant worlds and civilizations. She saw the birth and death of stars, the dance of galaxies, and the secrets of dark matter.

The visions faded, leaving Emilia breathless and awestruck. She knew that she had been given a great gift, a glimpse into the underlying fabric of the universe.

Dr. Erso smiled, her eyes shining with excitement. "We did it, Emilia. We cracked the code."

Together, they began to harness the power of quantum energy, using it to create innovative technologies that could change the course of human history.

But as they worked, Emilia began to realize that they were not alone. A mysterious organization, known only as "The Shadow Syndicate," was watching their every move.

Emilia's instincts told her that The Shadow Syndicate was dangerous, that they would stop at nothing to claim the power of quantum energy for themselves.

She knew that she and Dr. Erso had to be careful, that they had to protect their research at all costs.

As they worked tirelessly to advance their research, Emilia couldn't shake the feeling that they were being watched, that The Shadow Syndicate was waiting for the perfect moment to strike.

And then, one fateful night, Emilia's worst fears were realized. The Shadow Syndicate launched a surprise attack on their research facility, seeking to steal the quantum orb and claim its power for themselves.

Emilia and Dr. Erso fought bravely, but they were outnumbered and outgunned. Just when all seemed lost, Emilia remembered the power of the Celestial Map, the ancient artefact that had started her journey.

With a surge of adrenaline, Emilia activated the map, unleashing a blast of energy that repelled the attackers and sent them fleeing in disarray.

As the dust settled, Emilia and Dr. Erso stood victorious, but they knew that their work was far from over. They had to continue their research, to push the boundaries of what was possible with quantum energy.

And they had to be vigilant, for they knew that The Shadow Syndicate would not give up easily. Emilia's journey was far from over, and the fate of the galaxy hung in the balance.

As the days passed, Emilia and Dr. Erso worked tirelessly to advance their research. They knew that The Shadow Syndicate was still out there, waiting for an opportunity to strike.

One night, as they worked late in the lab, Emilia heard a faint noise coming from the shadows. She turned to see a figure emerging from the darkness.

It was a woman with piercing green eyes and long, flowing hair. She was dressed in a black jumpsuit, and a silver pendant glinted in the light.

"Who are you?" Emilia asked, her heart racing.

"My name is Aria," the woman replied, her voice low and mysterious. "I'm here to help you, Emilia. I know about The Shadow Syndicate, and I know about your research."

Emilia's instincts told her to trust Aria, but she was cautious. "What do you know about The Shadow Syndicate?" she asked.

Aria hesitated, then said, "I used to work for them. I was a scientist, but I realized that their goals were not aligned with mine. I want to help you stop them."

Dr. Erso looked at Aria with a sceptical eye. "How do we know we can trust you?" she asked.

Aria smiled. "You don't. But I'm willing to prove myself. I have information that can help you advance your research and stay one step ahead of The Shadow Syndicate."

Emilia and Dr. Erso exchanged a glance. They knew that they needed all the help they could get.

"Okay," Emilia said finally. "We'll listen to what you have to say."

Aria nodded, and began to explain her plan. Emilia and Dr. Erso listened intently, their minds racing with the possibilities.

As they talked, Emilia realized that Aria was more than just a scientist. She was a warrior, a fighter who had dedicated her life to taking down The Shadow Syndicate.

And Emilia knew that she had found a valuable ally in her quest to shape the future of the galaxy.

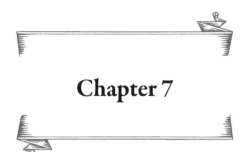

Chapter 7

Emilia, Dr. Erso, and Aria worked tirelessly to advance their research and stay ahead of The Shadow Syndicate. They knew that their work had the potential to change the course of human history, and they were determined to see it through.

As they worked, Emilia began to realize that Aria was more than just a scientist. She was a warrior, a fighter who had dedicated her life to taking down The Shadow Syndicate.

"Aria, what's your story?" Emilia asked one night, as they worked late in the lab.

Aria hesitated, then said, "I used to work for The Shadow Syndicate. I was a scientist, but I realized that their goals were not aligned with mine. I wanted to use my knowledge to help humanity, not control it."

Emilia nodded, understanding. "What made you leave?"

Aria's eyes flashed with anger. "I discovered that they were experimenting on innocent people. I couldn't be a part of that, so I left."

Emilia's heart went out to Aria. She knew that it couldn't have been easy to leave The Shadow Syndicate.

"What made you come here?" Emilia asked.

Aria smiled. "I heard about your research. I knew that it had the potential to change the world, and I wanted to be a part of it."

Emilia nodded, grateful for Aria's help. She knew that they made a good team.

As they continued their research, Emilia began to realize that Aria was not just a scientist, but a warrior. She was trained in hand-to-hand combat and was an expert in quantum technology.

"Aria, you're a warrior," Emilia said one night, as they worked late in the lab.

Aria nodded, her eyes flashing with pride. "I am. I've dedicated my life to taking down The Shadow Syndicate."

Emilia nodded, understanding. She knew that Aria was a valuable ally in their quest to shape the future of the galaxy.

As they delved deeper into their research, Emilia, Dr. Erso, and Aria began to notice strange occurrences around them. Equipment would malfunction, and strange noises could be heard coming from the shadows.

At first, they dismissed it as mere coincidence, but as the events grew more frequent and intense, they knew they had to investigate further.

One night, as they worked late in the lab, they heard a loud crash coming from the storage room. They rushed to the scene, finding that several crates had been knocked over, and strange symbols were etched into the walls.

Aria's eyes widened as she examined the symbols. "This is Shadow Syndicate code," she whispered. "They're trying to send us a message."

Emilia's heart raced as she realized the implications. "We need to get to the bottom of this," she said, determination in her voice.

Dr. Erso nodded, her eyes shining with a fierce light. "We'll increase security and keep working. We can't let them intimidate us."

As they continued their research, the strange occurrences grew more intense. Equipment would disappear, and strange creatures were seen lurking in the shadows.

Emilia knew that they were getting close to something big, something that The Shadow Syndicate didn't want them to discover.

One night, as they worked late in the lab, Emilia saw a figure lurking in the shadows. She knew that it was a Shadow Syndicate agent, and her heart raced with fear.

But as she looked closer, she saw that it was Aria, her eyes glowing with a fierce light.

"Aria, what's going on?" Emilia asked, confusion in her voice.

Aria stepped forward, her movements fluid and deadly. "I've been activated," she said, her voice low and menacing. "I'm a quantum warrior, and I'll do whatever it takes to protect you and our research."

Emilia's eyes widened as she realized the truth. Aria was not just a scientist, but a highly trained warrior, created to fight against The Shadow Syndicate.

As a quantum warrior, Aria possessed abilities that Emilia and Dr. Erso couldn't even begin to comprehend. She could manipulate matter at a molecular level, creating powerful force fields and projecting energy blasts from her hands.

With Aria by their side, the trio continued their research with renewed confidence. They worked tirelessly, pushing the boundaries of quantum technology and unlocking secrets that had been hidden for centuries.

But The Shadow Syndicate was not about to let them succeed without a fight. Agents began to appear in the lab, attempting to sabotage their equipment and steal their research.

Aria took point, using her abilities to deflect attacks and disarm the agents. Emilia and Dr. Erso worked in tandem, using their knowledge of quantum mechanics to outsmart the agents and stay one step ahead.

As the battles grew more intense, Emilia began to realize that Aria was not just a warrior - she was a guardian, sworn to protect the innocent and defend the truth.

And Emilia knew that she had found a true ally in Aria, one who would stand by her side no matter what dangers lay ahead.

Together, the trio pressed on, driven by their quest for knowledge and their determination to shape the future of the galaxy.

But little did they know, The Shadow Syndicate had one final trick up its sleeve - a weapon so powerful, it could destroy entire star systems.

And Emilia, Dr. Erso, and Aria were the only ones who could stop it.

Chapter 8

Emilia, Dr. Erso, and Aria stood at the threshold of a new discovery, one that could change the course of human history. They had unlocked the secrets of quantum technology, and now they were ready to unveil their findings to the world.

But as they prepared to share their research, they received a mysterious message from an unknown source. The message was simple yet ominous: "The Shadow Syndicate will stop at nothing to claim the quantum prophecy for themselves."

Emilia's heart raced as she realized the implications. The Shadow Syndicate would do anything to get their hands on the quantum technology, and she knew that she and her team were in grave danger.

Dr. Erso's eyes narrowed as she examined the message. "This is no ordinary threat," she said. "We must take action immediately."

Aria nodded in agreement. "I'll increase security and prepare for any eventuality."

Emilia took a deep breath and steeled herself for what was to come. She knew that they had to share their research with the world, no matter the risk.

And so, they went ahead with their plan, unveiling the quantum prophecy to a stunned audience. The reaction was overwhelming, with some hailing them as heroes and others condemning them as villains.

But Emilia knew that they had done the right thing. They had unlocked the secrets of the universe, and now it was up to humanity to use that knowledge for the greater good.

As they basked in the glory of their discovery, Emilia couldn't shake off the feeling that they were being watched. She knew that The Shadow Syndicate was still out there, waiting for their chance to strike.

And then, just as they were about to leave the stage, Emilia saw him - a tall, imposing figure with eyes that seemed to bore into her soul.

"Who is that?" Emilia whispered to Aria, her heart racing with fear.

Aria's expression turned grim. "That's the leader of The Shadow Syndicate. And he's not here to congratulate you."

The leader of The Shadow Syndicate, a man known only as "The Archon," stepped forward, his eyes fixed intently on Emilia. "You have something that belongs to us," he said, his voice dripping with malice.

Emilia stood tall, her heart pounding in her chest. "We've done nothing wrong," she said, her voice steady.

The Archon sneered. "You've unlocked the secrets of the quantum prophecy. That's something we've been searching for centuries."

Dr. Erso stepped forward, her eyes flashing with defiance. "We'll never let you have it," she said.

The Archon laughed. "We'll see about that," he said, snapping his fingers.

Suddenly, the room was filled with Shadow Syndicate agents, their guns drawn. Emilia, Dr. Erso, and Aria were surrounded.

"You have two choices," The Archon said. "Hand over the research, or die."

Emilia knew they had to act fast. She nodded to Aria, who sprang into action, using her quantum powers to disarm the agents and create a diversion.

In the chaos that followed, Emilia and Dr. Erso managed to escape, but they knew it was only a temporary reprieve. The Shadow Syndicate would stop at nothing to get what they wanted.

As they fled, Emilia realized that the quantum prophecy was more than just a discovery - it was a weapon, one that could change the course of human history. And she was determined to use it to bring down The Shadow Syndicate once and for all.

But as they ran, Emilia couldn't shake off the feeling that they were being herded towards a trap. The Shadow Syndicate seemed to be always one step ahead, and Emilia knew that their next move would be their most dangerous yet.

As they navigated through the winding streets of the city, Emilia's mind raced with thoughts of their next move. They had to get the research to a safe place, but where? The Shadow Syndicate seemed to have eyes and ears everywhere.

Dr. Erso noticed Emilia's distress and placed a reassuring hand on her shoulder. "We'll figure it out," she said. "We always do."

Aria, who had been scouting ahead, suddenly stopped and turned to face them. "Wait," she whispered. "Do you hear that?"

Emilia and Dr. Erso strained their ears, and soon they heard it too - the sound of footsteps, growing louder with each passing second.

"It's them," Aria said, her eyes flashing with warning. "We have to move, now!"

They quickly ducked into a nearby alleyway, their hearts pounding in unison. Emilia's mind raced with fear - what if they got caught? What if The Shadow Syndicate got their hands on the research?

As they caught their breath, Emilia realized that the alleyway was a dead end. They were trapped.

But Aria was already on the move, using her quantum powers to create a new path where none existed. Emilia and Dr. Erso followed close behind, their hearts filled with awe and gratitude.

As they emerged on the other side of the alleyway, Emilia saw a glimmer of hope. They might just make it out of this alive.

But The Shadow Syndicate was relentless, and Emilia knew that their next move would be their most dangerous yet. She steeled herself for what was to come, knowing that the fate of humanity hung in the balance.

As they ran, Emilia's mind raced with thoughts of their next move. They had to get the research to a safe place, but where? The Shadow Syndicate seemed to have eyes and ears everywhere.

Suddenly, Aria stopped and turned to face them. "Wait," she said, her eyes scanning the surrounding area. "I think I see a way out."

Emilia and Dr. Erso followed her gaze, and soon they saw it too - a small opening in the wall, just big enough for them to squeeze through.

"Quickly," Aria said, her voice low and urgent. "We have to move now."

They squeezed through the opening, finding themselves in a narrow, dimly lit tunnel. Emilia's heart raced as they made their way through the tunnel, the sound of The Shadow Syndicate's agents growing fainter with each step.

Finally, they emerged on the other side, gasping for air. Emilia looked around, taking in their surroundings. They were in a small, abandoned warehouse, the walls lined with crates and boxes.

"Where are we?" Emilia asked, her voice barely above a whisper.

Aria smiled. "Safe house," she said. "For now."

Dr. Erso nodded, her eyes scanning the area. "We need to get the research to a safe place," she said. "Somewhere The Shadow Syndicate can't find it."

Emilia nodded, her mind racing with thoughts of their next move. They had to protect the research, no matter what.

As they caught their breath, Emilia realized that they had made it out alive. But for how long? The Shadow Syndicate would stop at nothing to get what they wanted.

And Emilia knew that their next move would be their most dangerous yet.

Chapter 9

Emilia, Dr. Erso, and Aria made their way through the winding streets of the city, their hearts still racing from their narrow escape. They knew they had to find a safe place to hide the research, and fast.

As they turned a corner, Aria stopped suddenly, her eyes fixed on a nondescript building. "Here," she said, her voice low. "This is the place."

Emilia and Dr. Erso exchanged a sceptical glance, but Aria was already moving towards the entrance. They followed her, finding themselves in a dimly lit hallway.

The air was thick with the scent of chemicals and something else... something sweet. Emilia's nose wrinkled in distaste.

Aria led them deeper into the building, finally stopping at a door marked "Authorized Personnel Only". She produced a key card and swiped it through the reader.

The door slid open, revealing a state-of-the-art laboratory. Emilia's eyes widened as she took in the rows of workstations and cutting-edge equipment.

"Welcome to our hidden laboratory," Aria said, a hint of pride in her voice. "Here, we can finally analyse the research and unlock its secrets."

Dr. Erso's eyes sparkled with excitement. "This is incredible," she breathed. "We can finally make sense of the data."

Emilia nodded, her mind racing with possibilities. They were one step closer to unlocking the secrets of the quantum prophecy.

But as they began their work, Emilia couldn't shake off the feeling that they were being watched. She glanced around the laboratory, but saw nothing out of the ordinary.

Still, the feeling persisted. And Emilia knew that in their line of work, paranoia was a survival instinct.

As they delved deeper into the research, Emilia's unease grew. She couldn't shake off the feeling that they were being watched, and the air in the laboratory seemed to vibrate with an otherworldly energy.

Dr. Erso and Aria were too engrossed in their work to notice, but Emilia's instincts screamed warning. She tried to focus on the data, but her eyes kept darting towards the shadows.

Suddenly, a faint hum filled the air, and the equipment began to malfunction. Emilia's heart raced as she realized that they were not alone in the laboratory.

"Aria, Dr. Erso, we need to get out of here, now!" Emilia warned, her voice low and urgent.

But it was too late. The hum grew louder, and the air seemed to ripple with an invisible force. Emilia felt herself being pulled towards the centre of the laboratory, as if by an unseen magnet.

Dr. Erso and Aria were similarly affected, their eyes wide with fear as they stumbled towards the heart of the lab.

And then, everything went white.

Emilia's vision cleared to find herself in a vast, cavernous space. The laboratory was gone, replaced by an endless expanse of glittering stars.

A figure approached her, its features indistinct in the dazzling light.

"Welcome, Emilia," the figure said, its voice like a gentle breeze. "I have been waiting for you."

Emilia's heart pounded in her chest. Who was this mysterious being, and what did they want with her?

The being drew closer, its features slowly taking shape. Emilia saw that it was a woman with long, flowing hair and eyes that shone like stars.

"Who are you?" Emilia asked, her voice barely above a whisper.

"I am the Guardian of the Quantum Prophecy," the woman replied, her voice like music. "And you, Emilia, are the chosen one."

Emilia's mind raced with questions, but the Guardian raised a hand, forestalling her.

"You have been brought here for a purpose," the Guardian said. "The quantum prophecy is not just a theory - it is a reality, and you are the key to unlocking it."

Emilia felt a surge of excitement mixed with fear. What did the Guardian mean? And what lay ahead?

The Guardian's eyes seemed to bore into Emilia's soul. "Are you ready to embrace your destiny?" she asked.

Emilia took a deep breath and nodded. She was ready to face whatever lay ahead.

The Guardian's eyes gleamed with approval. "Then let us begin," she said, her voice dripping with anticipation.

With a wave of her hand, the Guardian conjured up a shimmering portal. Emilia felt a thrill of excitement mixed with trepidation as she gazed into its depths.

"This is the gateway to the Quantum Realm," the Guardian explained, her voice filled with awe. "Here, the secrets of the prophecy await."

Emilia steeled herself and stepped forward, feeling the portal's energy envelop her like a warm embrace.

As she emerged on the other side, Emilia found herself in a realm beyond her wildest dreams. Stars and galaxies whirled around her, and the air vibrated with an otherworldly music.

The Guardian's voice echoed in her mind. "Behold, Emilia, the Quantum Realm. Here, the prophecy's secrets await your discovery."

Emilia's heart pounded with excitement. She knew that this was just the beginning of an incredible journey.

As Emilia explored the Quantum Realm, she encountered strange and wondrous creatures that defied explanation. There were beings made of pure energy, others that seemed to be crafted from the very fabric of space-time itself.

The Guardian's voice guided her through the realm, pointing out hidden wonders and secret dangers. Emilia's mind raced with questions, but the Guardian's answers only led to more mysteries.

Despite the strangeness of it all, Emilia felt a deep connection to the Quantum Realm. She began to realize that this was where the prophecy's secrets awaited, hidden in the very fabric of reality.

As she delved deeper, Emilia encountered a great crystal temple at the heart of the realm. The Guardian's voice whispered in her ear, "Here lies the key to unlocking the prophecy's secrets."

Emilia's heart pounded with excitement and trepidation. What lay within the temple? Would she finally uncover the truth about the prophecy?

With a deep breath, Emilia stepped into the temple, ready to face whatever lay ahead.

Chapter 10

Emilia stepped into the crystal temple, her eyes adjusting to the dazzling light within. The air was filled with an otherworldly music, and the walls seemed to hum with energy.

The Guardian's voice echoed in her mind, "Here lies the heart of the Quantum Realm. Listen to the whispers of the crystal, and you shall uncover the secrets of the prophecy."

Emilia approached the central crystal, feeling its power coursing through her veins. As she touched its surface, visions began to flood her mind - images of distant worlds, ancient civilizations, and mysterious technologies.

The visions faded, leaving Emilia breathless and bewildered. But as she looked deeper into the crystal, she saw a glimmer of understanding.

"The prophecy is not just a prediction," she realized. "It's a key to unlocking the secrets of the universe."

Suddenly, the temple began to shake, and the music reached a fever pitch. Emilia stumbled, losing her balance.

The Guardian's voice cried out in warning, "Emilia, beware! The temple is collapsing. You must escape, now!"

Emilia turned to flee, but it was too late. The temple imploded, and everything went white.

When Emilia came to, she found herself back in the laboratory, the research team staring at her in concern.

"Emilia, what happened?" Dr. Erso asked, rushing to her side.

Emilia struggled to speak, her mind reeling from the experience. "The prophecy... the Quantum Realm... I saw the secrets of the universe."

Aria's eyes widened in awe. "You unlocked the prophecy's secrets?"

Emilia nodded, still dazed. "But at what cost? The temple collapsed. Did I trigger something?"

Dr. Erso's face turned grave. "We must analyse the data. Emilia, you may have unleashed a power beyond our control."

As the team scrambled to analyse the data, Emilia's mind raced with questions. What had she unleashed? And what did it mean for the future?

Dr. Erso's voice broke through her thoughts. "Emilia, we're reading an energy signature unlike anything we've seen before. It's as if the Quantum Realm is bleeding into our reality."

Aria's eyes sparkled with excitement. "This could be the discovery of a lifetime!"

But Emilia's gut warned her of danger. "We need to be careful. We don't know what we're dealing with."

Suddenly, the laboratory equipment began to malfunction, and the air seemed to distort. Emilia felt a strange energy building up inside her.

"Guys, I think we have a problem," she warned, her voice trembling.

And then, Emilia vanished.

The team stared in shock, unsure of what had just happened. Had Emilia been transported to another dimension?

Dr. Erso's face turned pale. "We have to find her. Now."

Aria nodded, determination etched on her face. "We'll search every corner of the Quantum Realm if we have to."

Dr. Erso and Aria frantically searched for Emilia, scouring the laboratory and the surrounding areas. But she was nowhere to be found.

THE TIME KEEPER'S QUEST

"We need to think this through," Dr. Erso said, her voice laced with concern. "Emilia was experimenting with the Quantum Realm. Maybe she got pulled into a parallel dimension."

Aria's eyes widened. "But which one? There are infinite possibilities!"

Dr. Erso's face set in determination. "We'll have to use the research we've gathered and try to track her down."

As they pored over the data, Emilia found herself in a strange, unfamiliar world. The sky was a deep purple, and the trees were a vibrant green. She saw creatures unlike any she had ever imagined, with iridescent wings and shimmering scales.

A figure approached her - a woman with long, flowing hair and eyes that seemed to see right through her.

"Welcome, Emilia," the woman said, her voice like music. "I have been waiting for you."

Emilia's mind raced with questions, but the woman simply smiled and took her hand.

"Come," she said. "Let me show you the wonders of this world."

As Emilia followed the woman, she realized that this was just the beginning of an incredible journey. She would encounter strange creatures, unexpected allies, and unimaginable challenges.

But she was ready. For Emilia knew that she had the power to shape her own destiny - and the fate of the multiverse.

As Emilia explored this new world, she encountered a strange creature with the ability to manipulate time. The creature, who introduced himself as the Timekeeper, revealed that Emilia had been brought to this world for a specific purpose.

"The fabric of reality is threatened," the Timekeeper explained, his voice grave. "A rogue entity is attempting to tear apart the multiverse. You, Emilia, have the power to stop it."

Emilia's mind reeled as she struggled to comprehend the enormity of the task ahead. But the Timekeeper's words echoed in her mind:

"You have the power to shape your own destiny - and the fate of the multiverse."

With newfound determination, Emilia accepted the challenge. She embarked on a perilous journey across dimensions, gathering allies and uncovering hidden secrets.

Meanwhile, Dr. Erso and Aria were frantically searching for Emilia, their efforts hindered by the increasingly unstable fabric of reality.

"We have to find her before it's too late," Dr. Erso urged, her voice laced with worry.

Aria nodded, her eyes fixed on the data streaming across her screen. "I think I've found a way to track her. Let's move!"

As they raced against time, Emilia confronted the rogue entity - a being of pure energy with the power to destroy entire universes.

"You're too late," the entity sneered, its voice like thunder. "The multiverse will soon be mine to command."

Emilia stood firm, her heart pounding in her chest. "I won't let that happen," she declared, her voice steady.

And with that, the battle for the multiverse began.

The battle raged on, Emilia harnessing her powers to create miniature black holes and quantum entanglements to slow down the entity's advance. But the entity was relentless, its energy output increasing with each passing moment.

Just when it seemed like all hope was lost, Dr. Erso and Aria burst into the scene, their equipment blazing with energy.

"We've got your back, Emilia!" Dr. Erso shouted, firing a beam of particles that disrupted the entity's field.

Aria followed up with a blast of quantum fluctuations, creating a localized distortion that sent the entity stumbling back.

Emilia seized the opportunity, channelling her powers into a massive quantum leap that sent her hurtling towards the entity.

The two collided in a spectacular display of energy and matter, their powers locked in a struggle that shook the very foundations of the multiverse.

And then, in an instant, it was over. The entity dissipated, its energy dispersing across the dimensions.

Emilia stood victorious, her powers spent but her spirit unbroken. Dr. Erso and Aria rushed to her side, relief etched on their faces.

"We did it," Emilia said, her voice barely above a whisper. "We saved the multiverse."

But as they celebrated their victory, a strange glow began to emanate from the quantum realm. A new threat was emerging, one that would require Emilia's powers once again.

Chapter 11

Emilia, Dr. Erso, and Aria returned to their laboratory, exhausted but triumphant. They had saved the multiverse from the rogue entity, but they knew that their work was far from over.

As they analysed the data from their recent battle, Emilia began to notice a strange pattern. The quantum fluctuations that had powered her abilities were growing stronger, as if she was tapping into a deeper well of energy.

"Guys, I think I'm onto something," Emilia said, her eyes fixed on the data streaming across her screen. "My powers are evolving. I can feel it."

Dr. Erso and Aria exchanged a knowing glance. "That's not all," Dr. Erso said, her voice measured. "We've detected a new anomaly in the quantum realm. It's calling to you, Emilia."

Emilia's heart raced as she realized what was happening. "It's time for the next leap," she said, her voice firm.

And with that, Emilia stepped into the unknown, ready to face whatever challenges lay ahead.

As Emilia embraced the anomaly, she felt her powers surging to new heights. The quantum fluctuations intensified, and her connection to the multiverse deepened.

Dr. Erso and Aria watched in awe as Emilia's body began to shimmer, her molecular structure blurring. "She's transcending space-time!" Dr. Erso exclaimed.

THE TIME KEEPER'S QUEST

Aria's eyes sparkled with wonder. "She's becoming one with the multiverse!"

Emilia's consciousness expanded, encompassing infinite possibilities. She saw the threads of reality, the hidden patterns that governed existence.

With this newfound understanding, Emilia reached out to the anomaly, merging with its energy. The laboratory around her dissolved, replaced by a realm beyond human comprehension.

In this mystical realm, Emilia encountered beings of pure energy, ancient sages who possessed secrets of the cosmos.

"Welcome, Emilia," one of the sages said, its voice like a gentle breeze. "We have awaited your arrival. You have the power to harmonize the multiverse."

Emilia's heart swelled with purpose. "I'm ready," she said, her voice filled with conviction.

And so, Emilia embarked on a quest to balance the multiverse, armed with her newfound powers and the wisdom of the ancient sages.

As Emilia journeyed through the mystical realm, she encountered a realm of chronal energies, where time itself was woven into fabric. She saw the tapestry of existence, with threads of past, present, and future intertwined.

A figure emerged from the shadows - a master weaver of time. "Emilia, you have been chosen to repair the fabric of chronology," the weaver said, its voice like the ticking of a clock.

Emilia's mind raced with questions, but the weaver handed her a shuttle of pure energy. "Use this to mend the tears in the fabric. Time is unravelling, and the multiverse is at risk."

With the shuttle in hand, Emilia set out to repair the damage. She navigated the labyrinthine paths of time, confronting rogue temporal entities and anomalies.

As she worked, Emilia discovered hidden aspects of her powers. She could manipulate time streams, creating localized eddies that allowed her to move through the fabric with precision.

With each repair, the fabric grew stronger, and the multiverse began to stabilize. Emilia's connection to the cosmic tapestry deepened, and she saw the intricate web of causality.

But as she approached the final tear, Emilia faced her greatest challenge yet - a being of pure entropy, hell-bent on unravelling the fabric of time itself.

As Emilia confronted the being of pure entropy, she felt the fabric of time trembling beneath her feet. The air was thick with the stench of decay, and the sky was a deep, burning crimson.

"You are the last obstacle to my ultimate goal," the being sneered, its voice like a rusty gate. "With your powers, I will unravel the very essence of existence."

Emilia stood firm, her determination fuelled by her connection to the cosmic tapestry. She raised her hands, and a blast of chronal energy shot forth, striking the being with precision.

But the being laughed, its form blurring as it absorbed the energy. "You think that's enough to stop me?" it taunted. "I have harnessed the power of a thousand black holes."

Undeterred, Emilia summoned a temporal storm, unleashing a maelstrom of chronal energy that threatened to consume the being. But it adapted, its form shifting to accommodate the assault.

The battle raged on, Emilia and the being exchanging blows that shook the fabric of time. Emilia's powers grew stronger with each passing moment, but the being seemed to draw energy from the very chaos it created.

As the fight reached its crescendo, Emilia realized that she needed a new approach. She focused her mind, reaching deep into the cosmic tapestry to find the thread of causality that bound the being to the fabric.

With a burst of insight, Emilia grasped the thread and pulled it taut, creating a temporal loop that trapped the being in a cycle of its own entropy.

The being howled in rage as Emilia closed the loop, banishing it from the fabric of time. The crimson sky faded to a soft blue, and the air was once again filled with the sweet scent of existence.

Emilia stood victorious, her powers spent but her spirit unbroken. She knew that she had saved the multiverse from the brink of destruction.

As she walked away from the battlefield, Emilia felt a gentle touch on her shoulder. She turned to see a figure cloaked in shadows.

"Well done, Emilia," the figure said, its voice like a soft breeze. "You have proven yourself a true guardian of the cosmic tapestry."

Emilia smiled, her heart filled with a sense of purpose. "I'm just getting started," she said, her eyes shining with determination.

And with that, Emilia continued her journey through the multiverse, ever vigilant and always ready to defend the fabric of existence.

As Emilia walked away from the battlefield, she felt a strange sensation in her pocket. She reached in and pulled out a small, glowing crystal.

"What's this?" she wondered, turning the crystal over in her hand.

Suddenly, the crystal began to pulse with energy, and Emilia felt herself being pulled into a vision.

She saw a great city, sprawling and beautiful, with towers that seemed to touch the sky. But as she looked closer, she saw that the city was in ruins, the buildings crumbling and the streets filled with debris.

Emilia's heart raced as she realized that this was a vision of the future, a future where the multiverse had been destroyed.

She saw herself standing in the midst of the ruins, surrounded by a group of survivors. They were looking to her for leadership, for a way to rebuild and start anew.

Emilia knew that she had to act, to use her powers to prevent this future from coming to pass. She focused her mind, reaching deep into the cosmic tapestry to find the threads of possibility.

And then, with a burst of energy, she saw it - a pathway through the multiverse, a way to avoid the destruction and build a new future.

Emilia's eyes snapped open, and she found herself back in the present, the crystal still clutched in her hand.

She knew what she had to do. She would follow the pathway, using her powers to guide her and protect the multiverse from those who would seek to destroy it.

Chapter 12

Emilia stood at the crossroads, the crystal held tightly in her hand. She could see the pathway unfolding before her, a shimmering thread of possibility that wound its way through the multiverse.

She took a deep breath, steeling herself for the journey ahead. She knew that she would face challenges and dangers, but she was ready.

With a sense of determination, Emilia stepped forward, onto the pathway. The world around her dissolved, replaced by a swirling vortex of colours and lights.

She felt herself being pulled through the multiverse, her consciousness expanding to encompass the infinite possibilities.

As she travelled, Emilia saw wonders and marvels beyond her wildest dreams. She saw stars and galaxies, worlds and civilizations beyond her own.

But she also saw the darkness, the shadows that sought to destroy the multiverse.

Emilia knew that she had to be brave, to face the darkness head-on. She focused her mind, reaching deep into the cosmic tapestry to find the threads of power.

And then, with a burst of energy, she saw it – a great and terrible foe, a being of darkness that sought to destroy the multiverse.

Emilia knew that she had to act, to use her powers to stop the being and save the multiverse. She steeled herself for the battle ahead, ready to face whatever challenges lay in store.

As Emilia approached the being of darkness, she felt a sense of trepidation. The being was enormous, its presence filling the vast expanse of the multiverse.

"You are the one who seeks to destroy the multiverse," Emilia said, her voice firm and resolute.

The being turned to her, its gaze like a cold, dark wind. "I am the one who will bring order to the multiverse," it replied, its voice like thunder.

Emilia knew that she had to act quickly. She raised her hands, and a blast of energy shot forth, striking the being with incredible force.

But the being was unfazed. It retaliated with a wave of darkness, a shadowy tendrils that sought to envelop Emilia.

Emilia dodged and weaved, avoiding the tendrils with her quick reflexes. She knew that she had to find a way to defeat the being, to save the multiverse from its destruction.

As she fought, Emilia realized that the being was not just a mindless monster. It had a purpose, a goal that drove it to destroy the multiverse.

"What is it that you seek?" Emilia asked, her voice firm.

The being hesitated, its gaze wavering. "I seek the secrets of the multiverse," it replied. "I seek the power to control all of existence."

Emilia knew that she had to stop the being, no matter what it took. She focused her mind, reaching deep into the cosmic tapestry to find the threads of power.

And then, with a burst of energy, she saw it – a way to defeat the being and save the multiverse.

Emilia harnessed the power of the cosmic tapestry, channelling it into a blast of energy that struck the being with incredible force. The being stumbled, its darkness receding as the light of the multiverse surged forth.

"You may have power," Emilia said, her voice firm, "but you will never have control. The multiverse is not yours to command."

The being snarled, its darkness flaring in anger. "You are no match for me," it spat. "I will crush you and your pitiful multiverse."

Emilia stood firm, her connection to the cosmic tapestry growing stronger with each passing moment. She knew that she had to end this battle, to stop the being before it was too late.

With a burst of inspiration, Emilia reached deep into the tapestry, finding a thread of possibility that she had not seen before. She pulled it forth, weaving it into a new pattern of reality.

The being howled in rage as Emilia's magic took effect. Its darkness began to unravel, its power fading as the multiverse itself turned against it.

"You may have sought to destroy the multiverse," Emilia said, her voice triumphant, "but in the end, it is you who will be destroyed."

And with that, the being of darkness dissipated, its essence torn apart by the very fabric of reality. Emilia stood victorious, her connection to the cosmic tapestry stronger than ever before.

But as she looked out into the multiverse, she knew that there would always be new challenges to face, new battles to fight.

As the being of darkness dissipated, Emilia felt a sense of relief wash over her. She had saved the multiverse from destruction, but she knew that her work was far from over.

She looked out into the vast expanse of the multiverse, her eyes scanning the infinite possibilities. She knew that there were still threats lurking in the shadows, waiting to strike.

But Emilia was ready. She had harnessed the power of the cosmic tapestry, and she knew that she could face whatever challenges came her way.

With a sense of determination, Emilia set off into the unknown, her heart filled with a sense of wonder and her spirit fuelled by her unwavering commitment to protect the multiverse.

As she journeyed deeper into the unknown, Emilia encountered strange and wondrous sights. She saw stars and galaxies, worlds and civilizations beyond her wildest dreams.

But she also saw the darkness, the shadows that sought to destroy all that was good. Emilia knew that she had to be vigilant, to always be prepared to face the challenges that lay ahead.

And so she travelled on, her heart filled with hope and her spirit fuelled by her determination to protect the multiverse.

As Emilia ventured deeper into the unknown, she stumbled upon a mysterious planet shrouded in an aura of secrecy. The planet's atmosphere was thick with an otherworldly energy, and Emilia could feel its power calling to her.

Without hesitation, Emilia descended onto the planet's surface, her senses on high alert. She navigated through the dense foliage, her heart pounding with anticipation.

Suddenly, a figure emerged from the shadows. It was a woman with long, flowing hair and piercing green eyes. She regarded Emilia with a curious expression.

"Welcome, Emilia," the woman said, her voice like music. "I have been expecting you. My name is Aria, and I possess knowledge that will aid you in your quest."

Emilia's eyes narrowed. "What knowledge?" she asked, her hand on the hilt of her sword.

Aria smiled. "The secrets of the cosmic tapestry. I can teach you how to harness its power and wield it against the forces of darkness."

Emilia's eyes widened. "You can teach me?" she repeated, her mind racing with possibilities.

Aria nodded. "But first, you must prove yourself worthy. I shall set you three trials. If you succeed, I will impart my knowledge to you."

Emilia steeled herself. "I'm ready. Let the trials begin."

And with that, Emilia embarked on a series of challenges that would test her courage, wit, and strength.

Chapter 13

Emilia stood before Aria, her heart pounding with anticipation. "The first trial is the Labyrinth of Reflections," Aria said, her eyes glinting with a hint of mischief. "You must navigate its paths and confront your deepest fears."

Emilia steeled herself and entered the labyrinth. The air was thick with the scent of smoke and mirrors, and Emilia's senses were disoriented. She wandered the twisting paths, encountering illusions that seemed all too real.

Suddenly, a figure emerged from the shadows. It was a dark version of Emilia herself, its eyes blazing with malevolence.

"You are weak," the dark Emilia sneered. "You will never succeed."

Emilia drew her sword, its blade shimmering with light. "I am not afraid of you," she said, her voice steady.

The dark Emilia attacked, and Emilia parried its blows, her heart pounding in her chest. But as the battle raged on, Emilia realized that her foe was not just a physical enemy - it was a manifestation of her own doubts and fears.

With a surge of determination, Emilia confronted her dark self, embracing her flaws and weaknesses. The dark Emilia dissipated, and Emilia emerged victorious.

Aria awaited her outside the labyrinth, a nod of approval on her face. "Well done, Emilia. You have passed the first trial."

Emilia breathed a sigh of relief. "What's the next trial?" she asked, her spirit eager for the challenge.

"The second trial is the Caverns of Whispers," Aria said, her eyes glinting with a hint of mystery. "You must listen to the whispers of the ancients and uncover the secrets of the cosmic tapestry."

Emilia ventured into the Caverns of Whispers, her heart racing with anticipation. The air was thick with the scent of aged dust and forgotten knowledge. She wandered the winding tunnels, her ears straining to discern the whispers of the ancients.

As she walked, the whispers grew louder, a cacophony of ancient secrets and mysterious prophecies. Emilia's mind reeled, struggling to decipher the meaning behind the whispers.

Suddenly, a figure emerged from the shadows. It was an ancient sage, its eyes aglow with wisdom.

"Listen well, Emilia," the sage said, its voice like a gentle breeze. "The whispers hold the secrets of the cosmic tapestry. But you must listen with your heart, not just your mind."

Emilia nodded, her heart open and receptive. And as she listened, the whispers began to make sense, revealing hidden patterns and ancient truths.

With a surge of understanding, Emilia grasped the secrets of the cosmic tapestry. She saw the interconnectedness of all things, the delicate balance of the universe.

Aria awaited her outside the caverns, a smile of approval on her face. "Well done, Emilia. You have passed the second trial."

Emilia breathed a sigh of accomplishment. "What's the final trial?" she asked, her spirit eager for the challenge.

"The final trial is the Mirror of the Soul," Aria said, her eyes glinting with a hint of mystery. "You must confront your deepest desires and fears, and emerge victorious."

Emilia stood before the Mirror of the Soul, her heart pounding with anticipation. The mirror's surface was smooth and unblemished, reflecting her image with perfect clarity.

"Look into the mirror, Emilia," Aria said, her voice gentle. "Confront your deepest desires and fears. Only then can you emerge victorious."

Emilia took a deep breath and gazed into the mirror. At first, she saw only her own reflection. But as she looked deeper, the image began to shift and change.

She saw herself as a child, playing with her parents in a sun-drenched field. She saw herself as a young woman, standing proudly beside her mentor, Eira. And she saw herself as a warrior, battling against the forces of darkness.

But as the visions faded, Emilia saw a darker reflection emerge. She saw herself consumed by ambition, sacrificing all that was dear to her in pursuit of power. She saw herself lost in the shadows, forever trapped in the darkness.

Emilia recoiled, horrified by the reflection. But as she looked closer, she saw something else. She saw a glimmer of light, a spark of hope that even in the darkest depths, there was always a way forward.

With a newfound understanding, Emilia reached out and touched the mirror. The surface rippled, like water disturbed by a stone. And as the ripples faded, Emilia saw a new reflection emerge.

She saw herself standing tall, her heart filled with light and her spirit burning with determination. She saw herself as a true warrior, armed with the power of the cosmic tapestry and the wisdom of the ancients.

Aria smiled, her eyes shining with approval. "Well done, Emilia. You have passed the final trial."

Emilia breathed a sigh of relief, her heart filled with a sense of accomplishment. She knew that she had faced her deepest fears and emerged victorious.

And as she turned to leave, Emilia saw a figure waiting for her in the shadows. It was Eira, her mentor and friend.

"I am proud of you, Emilia," Eira said, her voice warm".

"Emilia, you have proven yourself to be a true warrior," Eira said, her eyes shining with pride. "You have faced your fears and emerged victorious. Now, it is time for you to receive your reward."

Emilia's heart raced with excitement as Eira led her to a hidden chamber deep within the caverns. Inside, she found a beautiful sword with a gleaming silver blade and a hilt adorned with precious gems.

"This is the Sword of Light," Eira said, presenting the sword to Emilia. "It is a powerful weapon, forged from the very essence of the cosmic tapestry. With this sword, you will be able to vanquish any darkness and bring light to even the most shadowy of places."

Emilia took the sword, feeling its power coursing through her veins. She knew that this was a momentous occasion, one that marked a new chapter in her journey as a warrior.

As she held the sword aloft, the caverns were filled with a brilliant light, and Emilia felt herself being lifted off the ground. She was surrounded by a halo of energy, and she knew that she was being transformed by the power of the sword.

When the light faded, Emilia found herself back in the chamber, the sword still clutched in her hand. But something was different. She felt stronger, more confident, and more determined than ever before.

"Thank you, Eira," Emilia said, her voice filled with gratitude. "I will not fail you or the cosmic tapestry. I will use this sword to bring light to the darkness and to defend all that is good."

Eira smiled, her eyes shining with pride. "I know you will, Emilia. You are a true warrior, and I have no doubt that you will fulfil your destiny."

And with that, Emilia left the caverns, ready to face whatever challenges lay ahead, armed with the power of the Sword of Light.

Chapter 14

Emilia ventured deeper into the unknown, the Sword of Light by her side. She had been traveling for days, and the landscape had grown increasingly treacherous. But she pressed on, driven by a sense of purpose.

As she crested a ridge, Emilia saw it - a sprawling city, hidden away in the heart of the mountains. The buildings were ancient, covered in vines and moss, and the air was thick with the scent of decay.

Emilia's heart raced as she approached the city. She could feel a powerful energy emanating from within, a energy that seemed to be calling to her.

As she explored the city, Emilia began to uncover its secrets. She found ancient artefacts, mysterious devices, and cryptic writings on the walls. It was as if the city was trying to tell her something, but she couldn't quite decipher the message.

Suddenly, Emilia heard a noise behind her. She turned to see a figure emerging from the shadows - a woman with long, flowing hair and piercing green eyes.

"Welcome, Emilia," the woman said, her voice low and mysterious. "I have been waiting for you. My name is Lyra, and I am the guardian of this city."

Emilia's hand instinctively went to the hilt of her sword. "What do you want from me?" she asked, her eyes narrowing.

Lyra smiled, her eyes glinting with amusement. "Oh, Emilia. I want to show you the secrets of the city. And perhaps... perhaps we can help each other."

And with that, Emilia followed Lyra into the heart of the city, ready to uncover its secrets.

As Emilia followed Lyra through the winding streets of the lost city, she couldn't help but feel a sense of wonder. The buildings seemed to stretch on forever, each one more intricate and beautiful than the last.

"What is this place?" Emilia asked, her eyes wide with awe.

"It is the city of Eldarath," Lyra replied, her voice filled with a deep reverence. "A place of ancient power and knowledge."

As they walked, Emilia noticed that the city seemed to be shifting and changing around her. Buildings would disappear and reappear, and streets would twist and turn in impossible ways.

"How is this possible?" Emilia asked, her mind struggling to keep up.

"This city exists outside of the normal flow of time and space," Lyra explained. "It is a nexus point, a crossroads of dimensions and realities."

Emilia's mind reeled as she tried to comprehend the implications. "And what is your role in all of this?" she asked.

"I am the guardian of this city," Lyra replied. "I have sworn to protect its secrets and keep its power from falling into the wrong hands."

As they turned a corner, Emilia saw a massive stone door looming before them. It was adorned with intricate carvings and symbols of power.

"What lies beyond this door?" Emilia asked, her heart pounding with excitement.

"The heart of the city," Lyra replied. "And the source of its power."

With a wave of her hand, Lyra opened the door, revealing a chamber filled with a brilliant light. Emilia stepped forward, ready to face whatever lay ahead.

As Emilia stepped into the chamber, she was struck by the intensity of the light. It was as if the very essence of the city was concentrated in this one room. Lyra followed close behind, her eyes gleaming with a knowing light.

"The heart of the city is a powerful artefact," Lyra said, her voice barely above a whisper. "It holds the secrets of Eldarath and the key to unlocking its true potential."

Emilia's eyes adjusted slowly to the light, and she saw that the room was filled with a glittering crystal structure. It pulsed with energy, and Emilia could feel its power calling to her.

"This is the Crystal of Eldarath," Lyra said, her hand reaching out to touch the crystal. "It holds the essence of the city and the knowledge of the ancients."

As Lyra touched the crystal, the room began to shift and change around them. The walls dissolved, revealing a vast expanse of stars and galaxies. Emilia felt herself being pulled into the crystal, her mind expanding to comprehend the secrets of the universe.

"This is incredible," Emilia breathed, her mind reeling with the implications. "What secrets does it hold?"

"The secrets of creation and destruction," Lyra replied, her eyes gleaming with a fierce light. "The secrets of life and death. And the secrets of the cosmos itself."

Emilia's mind was racing with questions, but before she could ask any of them, Lyra spoke again.

"But beware, Emilia. The crystal is guarded by powerful entities who will stop at nothing to keep its secrets. Are you prepared to face what lies within?"

Emilia steeled herself, her heart pounding with excitement and a hint of fear. She knew that she had to uncover the secrets of the crystal, no matter what dangers lay ahead.

"I'm ready," Emilia said, her voice firm and resolute.

And with that, Lyra led Emilia deeper into the heart of the crystal.

As they journeyed deeper into the crystal, Emilia encountered strange and wondrous sights. She saw galaxies colliding, stars being born, and planets dying. She saw the dance of gravity and the song of the cosmos.

But she also saw darker things. She saw black holes devouring entire galaxies, and supernovae destroying entire star systems. She saw the destruction of worlds and the death of hope.

And through it all, Lyra was by her side, guiding her and explaining the secrets of the universe.

"This is the cosmos in all its glory," Lyra said, her voice filled with awe. "Beautiful and terrible, full of wonder and full of danger."

Emilia's mind was reeling with the implications. She had never imagined that the universe was so vast and complex.

"But what is the purpose of it all?" Emilia asked, her voice barely above a whisper.

"That is the greatest mystery of all," Lyra replied, her eyes gleaming with a fierce light. "The purpose of the universe is hidden, even from those who have spent centuries studying it. But I believe that it is connected to the heart of the crystal."

As they reached the centre of the crystal, Emilia saw a glowing orb of light. It pulsed with energy, and Emilia could feel its power calling to her.

"This is the Heart of Eldarath," Lyra said, her voice filled with reverence. "The source of all power and all knowledge."

Emilia reached out a trembling hand and touched the orb. And in that moment, she knew everything. She knew the secrets of the universe, the secrets of life and death, and the secrets of the cosmos.

But as she looked into the orb, Emilia saw something else. She saw a figure, tall and imposing, with eyes that burned with an inner fire.

"Who are you?" Emilia asked, her voice barely above a whisper.

"I am the Guardian of the Crystal," the figure replied, its voice like thunder. "And you, Emilia, are the chosen one. You have been chosen to wield the power of the crystal and to fulfil an ancient prophecy."

Emilia's mind reeled with the implications. She had never imagined that she was destined for something so great.

"What prophecy?" Emilia asked, her voice filled with wonder.

"The prophecy of the chosen one," the Guardian replied. "You are destined to save the universe from a great darkness that threatens to consume everything. Are you ready to accept this challenge?"

Chapter 15

Emilia's mind raced with questions as she listened to the Guardian's words. Save the universe? What did that even mean? And what darkness was threatening to consume everything?

"The prophecy speaks of a great evil that will soon be unleashed upon the universe," the Guardian explained, its voice grave. "An evil that will destroy entire galaxies and civilizations. But you, Emilia, have been chosen to stop it."

Emilia felt a surge of determination. She was ready to face whatever challenges lay ahead.

"Tell me more," Emilia said, her voice firm.

"The evil is known as the Shadow," the Guardian replied. "It is a powerful and malevolent force that has been growing in power for centuries. It will stop at nothing to consume everything in its path."

Emilia's heart raced with fear, but she steeled herself for the challenge.

"What must I do to stop it?" Emilia asked, her voice resolute.

"You must gather the three ancient artefacts," the Guardian replied. "The Sword of Light, the Shield of Courage, and the Crown of Wisdom. With these artefacts, you will have the power to defeat the Shadow and save the universe."

Emilia nodded, her mind racing with the task ahead.

"I'm ready," Emilia said, her voice firm. "Let's begin."

And with that, Emilia set off on her quest to gather the artefacts and save the universe from the Shadow.

As Emilia embarked on her perilous quest, she encountered a mystical being who revealed to her the first artefact's location. The being, known as the Keeper of the Sword, presented Emilia with a series of challenges that tested her courage, wit, and determination.

Emilia successfully completed the challenges and claimed the Sword of Light, feeling its power coursing through her veins. She then set out to find the Shield of Courage, facing treacherous landscapes and fending off formidable creatures along the way.

As she neared the shield's supposed location, Emilia encountered a wise old sage who offered to guide her through the treacherous terrain. Together, they navigated ancient ruins and solved cryptic puzzles, finally reaching the shield's resting place.

With the Shield of Courage in hand, Emilia felt an surge of confidence and bravery. She pressed on, determined to find the final artefact, the Crown of Wisdom.

Her journey took her to a mystical realm, where she encountered a enigmatic queen who possessed the crown. The queen presented Emilia with a series of riddles, each one more challenging than the last.

Emilia's wit and intuition served her well, and she solved the riddles, earning the queen's respect and the Crown of Wisdom. With all three artefacts in hand, Emilia felt an overwhelming sense of power and responsibility.

She knew that the Shadow was growing stronger by the minute and that she had to act swiftly to defeat it. Emilia steeled herself for the ultimate battle, ready to face whatever lay ahead. The fate of the universe rested on her shoulders, and she was determined to save it.

With the Crown of Wisdom securely in her possession, Emilia felt a sense of calm wash over her. She knew that the final battle was imminent, but she was ready. The artefacts hummed with power, and Emilia could feel their energy coursing through her veins.

As she stood before the Shadow's dark portal, Emilia steeled herself for the ultimate confrontation. The air grew thick with tension, and the ground trembled beneath her feet.

"You are a foolish mortal," the Shadow sneered, its voice like a cold wind. "You think you can defeat me? I am the darkness that consumes all!"

Emilia drew the Sword of Light, its blade shining brightly in the dim light. "I am not afraid of you," she said, her voice steady. "I have the power of the artefacts, and I will use them to vanquish you!"

The Shadow snarled, its darkness coalescing into a massive, tendrilled creature. Emilia raised the Shield of Courage, and a brilliant light burst forth, repelling the creature's attack.

With a swift motion, Emilia donned the Crown of Wisdom, and a surge of knowledge flooded her mind. She saw the Shadow's weakness and struck with precision, the Sword of Light slicing through the darkness like a beacon of hope.

The battle raged on, Emilia dodging and weaving between the Shadow's attacks, her artefacts shining brightly as she wielded them with grace and determination. Finally, with a triumphant cry, Emilia struck the final blow, banishing the Shadow back to the depths of the underworld.

As the darkness receded, Emilia stood victorious, her artefacts aglow with a soft, pulsing light. She knew that the universe was forever changed, and that she had become something more than just a mortal.

As the Shadow dissipated, Emilia felt a strange sensation wash over her. The artefacts, once humming with power, now seemed to be whispering secrets in her ear. She listened intently, and suddenly, the universe unfolded before her like a tapestry.

She saw the threads of fate connecting all living beings, and the delicate balance of the cosmos. Emilia realized that she had become a part of something much greater than herself, a guardian of the universe's harmony.

With this newfound understanding, Emilia set out to explore the mysteries of the cosmos. She travelled to distant planets, encountered strange creatures, and unravelled ancient mysteries. The artefacts guided her on her journey, revealing hidden truths and unseen wonders.

As Emilia delved deeper into the unknown, she discovered a hidden realm, a dimension parallel to her own. There, she met a being of pure energy, a guardian of the multiverse.

"You have been chosen to wield the artefacts," the being said, its voice like a symphony of stars. "But with great power comes great responsibility. Will you use your gifts to maintain balance and harmony, or will you let the universe fall into chaos?"

Emilia knew the answer, and with a determined heart, she accepted the challenge. And so, her epic journey continued, a never-ending quest to protect the universe and keep the artefacts' power in check.

Chapter 16

Emilia stood before the being of pure energy, her mind racing with questions. "What do you mean by 'maintain balance and harmony'?" she asked.

"The universe is a delicate web of threads," the being replied. "Every action, every decision, ripples across the fabric of space and time. You must use the artefacts to ensure that the ripples do not become waves of destruction."

Emilia nodded, determination burning within her. "I understand. But how do I do that?"

The being gestured, and a vision appeared before Emilia. She saw a great tapestry, woven from threads of light and darkness. "This is the fabric of the universe," the being said. "You must use the artefacts to weave a pattern of balance and harmony."

Emilia studied the tapestry, her mind racing with the complexity of the task. But she was ready to face the challenge. "I will do it," she said, her voice firm.

The being nodded, its energy pulsing with approval. "Then let us begin."

And with that, Emilia embarked on her new quest, using the artefacts to weave a pattern of balance and harmony across the universe. She travelled to distant galaxies, encountered strange creatures, and unravelled ancient mysteries. The artefacts guided her on her journey, revealing hidden truths and unseen wonders.

As Emilia worked to maintain the balance of the universe, she discovered a hidden threat. A dark force, known only as the Devourer, was consuming entire galaxies, leaving destruction in its wake.

Emilia knew she had to act fast. She gathered the artefacts and set out to confront the Devourer. The fate of the universe hung in the balance, and Emilia was the only one who could save it.

As Emilia journeyed through the galaxies, she encountered a mysterious figure known only as the Architect. He revealed to her that the Devourer was once a powerful civilization that had consumed itself in its quest for knowledge and power.

"The Devourer is a monster of their own creation," the Architect said, his voice laced with sorrow. "They sought to defy the laws of the universe and paid the price. Now, it hungers for destruction, leaving nothing but desolation in its wake."

Emilia's heart went out to the civilization that had fallen so far. She knew she had to stop the Devourer, but she also wanted to understand what had driven them to such destruction.

"What can I do to stop it?" Emilia asked the Architect.

"You must find the Echoes of Creation," he replied. "They hold the secrets of the universe and the key to defeating the Devourer."

Emilia's quest led her to the edges of the universe, where she encountered strange creatures and witnessed breath-taking wonders. She discovered hidden temples, ancient artefacts, and mysterious energies.

As she gathered the Echoes of Creation, Emilia began to understand the true nature of the universe. She saw the interconnectedness of all things and the delicate balance that sustained life.

With the Echoes in hand, Emilia faced the Devourer, her heart filled with compassion and her spirit burning with determination. She knew that she had the power to stop the destruction and restore balance to the universe.

The battle with the Devourer was fierce, but Emilia's resolve never wavered. She used the Echoes of Creation to weave a new pattern, one that would restore harmony to the universe.

As the Devourer dissipated into nothingness, Emilia felt a sense of pride and accomplishment. She had saved countless civilizations and restored balance to the universe.

But her journey was far from over. Emilia knew that there were more secrets to uncover, more mysteries to solve, and more adventures to be had. And so, she set off into the unknown.

As Emilia explored the mysteries of the universe, she stumbled upon an ancient civilization hidden deep within a nebula. The civilization, known as the Guardians of the Cosmos, possessed knowledge and power beyond her wildest dreams.

They revealed to Emilia that she was chosen to wield the Celestial Sceptre, a powerful artefact that could manipulate the very fabric of space and time. With the sceptre, Emilia could create entire galaxies or destroy them with a mere thought.

But the Guardians warned Emilia that the sceptre came with a great cost. Each use would drain her life force, and the power came with a terrible curse that would haunt her forever.

Emilia was torn. She knew the sceptre's power could benefit the universe, but she also feared its curse. As she grappled with the decision, a strange energy signature appeared on the horizon.

It was a being known as the Timekeeper, a powerful entity who controlled the flow of time itself. The Timekeeper revealed that Emilia's use of the Celestial Sceptre would disrupt the time stream, causing irreparable damage to the universe.

Emilia knew she had to make a choice. She could either wield the sceptre and risk destroying the universe or refuse its power and allow the cosmos to unfold naturally. The fate of the universe rested in her hands.

Emilia decided to refuse the power of the Celestial Sceptre, knowing that its curse and potential to disrupt the time stream were too great to risk. The Guardians of the Cosmos respected her decision and revealed a new path for her to follow.

They led her to a hidden chamber deep within their city, where a ancient artefact known as the Chronosphere awaited. The Chronosphere was a powerful device that allowed its user to manipulate time itself, but without the risks associated with the Celestial Sceptre.

With the Chronosphere, Emilia could travel through time, witness historic events, and even communicate with her past or future self. But she soon realized that changing events in the past would have unintended consequences on the present and future.

Emilia must now navigate the complexities of time travel, ensuring that her actions in the past do not disrupt the timeline. She will encounter strange creatures, witness pivotal moments in history, and uncover hidden secrets about the universe and herself.

As Emilia explores the mysteries of time, she begins to uncover a sinister plot to alter the course of history. A rogue time traveller seeks to erase entire civilizations from existence, and Emilia must stop them before it's too late.

With the Chronosphere as her tool and her wits as her guide, Emilia embarks on a thrilling adventure through time, racing against the clock to protect the universe and ensure its very survival.

Chapter 17

Emilia stood before the Chronosphere, her mind racing with the possibilities. She could travel anywhere in time, witness any event, and even meet her ancestors. But as she reached out to activate the device, a warning echoed in her mind.

"Remember, Emilia, every action in the past has consequences in the present and future," the Guardians of the Cosmos had cautioned. "Use your power wisely."

Emilia took a deep breath and focused on her destination: ancient Egypt during the reign of Ramses II. She had always been fascinated by the pyramids and the mysterious pharaohs who built them.

As the Chronosphere whirled to life, Emilia felt a strange sensation, like being pulled apart and put back together again. When she opened her eyes, she found herself standing amidst a bustling Egyptian market.

Camels and merchants crowded the streets, while the Great Pyramid loomed in the distance. Emilia marvelled at the sights and sounds, but her wonder was short-lived.

A figure emerged from the crowd, a young woman with a determined look in her eye. "You're the time traveller," she said, her voice low and urgent. "I've been waiting for you."

Emilia was taken aback. "Who are you?" she asked.

"I am Kiya, a priestess of the goddess Isis," the woman replied. "And I need your help to prevent a disaster that will destroy our civilization."

Emilia's mind raced with questions, but Kiya's words were laced with a sense of desperation. She knew she had to act quickly.

"What disaster?" Emilia asked, her heart pounding with anticipation.

"The pharaoh's advisor, a man named Ahmose, seeks to overthrow Ramses II and claim the throne for himself," Kiya explained. "But his actions will bring about a terrible curse that will destroy our land and our people."

Emilia knew she had to act fast. She could use the Chronosphere to prevent Ahmose's treachery, but at what cost? Changing events in the past was a delicate art, and Emilia knew that one misstep could have disastrous consequences.

Emilia knew that she had to be careful. She couldn't just rush into ancient Egyptian politics without understanding the consequences of her actions. She needed a plan.

"Kiya, can you tell me more about Ahmose and his plans?" Emilia asked, her mind racing with possibilities.

Kiya nodded, her eyes serious. "Ahmose is a cunning man. He has been secretly gathering support among the other advisors and nobles, whispering lies and half-truths about Ramses II. He claims that the pharaoh is weak and that Egypt needs a strong leader to survive."

Emilia's eyes narrowed. "And what about the curse? What kind of curse could possibly destroy an entire civilization?"

Kiya's voice dropped to a whisper. "The curse of the gods. Ahmose plans to desecrate the temples and steal the sacred artefacts. He believes that this will give him the power to control the gods themselves."

Emilia's heart raced with excitement and fear. She knew that she had to stop Ahmose, but she also knew that it wouldn't be easy. She would have to navigate the treacherous waters of ancient Egyptian politics, avoid detection by Ahmose's spies, and somehow prevent the curse from being unleashed.

As she pondered her next move, Emilia heard a faint rustling sound coming from the shadows. She turned to see a figure emerging from the darkness.

"Who are you?" Emilia asked, her hand instinctively reaching for the Chronosphere.

The figure stepped forward, revealing a tall, imposing man with piercing eyes. "I am Ani, a loyal servant of Ramses II. And I have been sent to warn you, Emilia."

Emilia's eyes narrowed. "Warn me about what?"

Ani's voice was low and urgent. "Ahmose's plans are more sinister than you think. He has made a pact with a dark force, a being from the underworld who will grant him immense power in exchange for his soul."

Emilia's heart raced with excitement and fear. She knew that she had to act fast. She couldn't let Ahmose unleash a dark force upon the world.

Emilia knew she had to make a decision quickly. She couldn't let Ahmose unleash a dark force upon the world, but she also knew that stopping him wouldn't be easy.

"Ani, can you tell me more about this dark force?" Emilia asked, her mind racing with possibilities.

Ani nodded, his eyes serious. "It's an ancient being from the underworld, a creature of immense power and destruction. Ahmose believes that with its help, he can conquer all of Egypt and rule with absolute power."

Emilia's heart raced with excitement and fear. She knew that she had to stop Ahmose, but she also knew that it wouldn't be easy. She would have to use all her skills and cunning to outwit him and prevent the curse from being unleashed.

As she pondered her next move, Emilia heard a faint rustling sound coming from the shadows. She turned to see a figure emerging from the darkness.

"Who are you?" Emilia asked, her hand instinctively reaching for the Chronosphere.

The figure stepped forward, revealing a mysterious woman with piercing green eyes. "I am Nephthys, goddess of death and magic. And I have come to offer you my help, Emilia."

Emilia's eyes narrowed. "Why would you help me?"

Nephthys smiled, her lips curving upwards. "Because I have a stake in this too, Emilia. Ahmose's actions will not only destroy Egypt, but also upset the balance of the underworld. I cannot allow that to happen."

Emilia hesitated, unsure if she could trust Nephthys. But she knew she needed all the help she could get.

"Okay, I accept your offer," Emilia said finally. "But I need to know more about Ahmose's plans. Can you tell me where he is now?"

Nephthys nodded, her eyes glinting with knowledge. "Ahmose is currently in the temple of Ptah, performing a dark ritual to summon the creature from the underworld."

Emilia's heart raced with excitement and fear. She knew she had to act fast. She couldn't let Ahmose unleash a dark force upon the world.

Chapter 18

Emilia, Ani, Kiya, and Nephthys approached the temple of Ptah with caution. They knew that Ahmose was performing a dark ritual inside, and they didn't want to be detected.

As they entered the temple, Emilia could feel the air thickening with anticipation. She knew that they were getting close to Ahmose.

Suddenly, they heard a loud chanting noise coming from the inner sanctum. Emilia recognized the words as an ancient spell of summoning.

"It's starting," Emilia whispered to her companions. "We have to act fast."

Ani drew his sword, while Kiya and Nephthys prepared their magic. Emilia readied the Chronosphere, her heart pounding with excitement and fear.

As they burst into the inner sanctum, Emilia saw Ahmose standing before a glowing portal. He was chanting loudly, his eyes closed in concentration.

"Stop him!" Emilia shouted, but Ahmose didn't flinch.

The creature from the underworld emerged from the portal, its eyes blazing with fury. Emilia knew they had to act fast.

As the creature emerged from the portal, Emilia felt a surge of energy emanating from it. She knew that she had to act fast, or risk being consumed by its power.

Ani charged forward, his sword flashing in the dim light of the temple. Kiya and Nephthys followed close behind, their magic swirling around them like a vortex.

Emilia raised the Chronosphere, its power coursing through her veins like liquid fire. She knew that she had to use it wisely, or risk unravelling the very fabric of time itself.

As the creature turned to face them, Emilia saw something that made her heart skip a beat. Ahmose was no longer in control - the creature had taken possession of his body, using him as a puppet to wreak havoc on the world.

"We have to stop Ahmose, not the creature!" Emilia shouted to her companions. "We need to break the curse that's controlling him!"

Ani nodded, his sword slicing through the air with deadly precision. Kiya and Nephthys adjusted their magic, focusing on Ahmose instead of the creature.

Emilia used the Chronosphere to create a temporal loop, reliving the same few seconds over and over. Each time, she tried something different, attempting to break the curse that held Ahmose in its grasp.

But the creature was powerful, and it would not give up easily. It fought back with all its might, summoning waves of dark energy to crash down on Emilia and her companions.

As the battle raged on, Emilia began to tire. She knew that she couldn't keep this up for much longer - the Chronosphere was draining her life force with each use.

Just when it seemed like all was lost, Nephthys stepped forward, her magic blazing with intensity. "I'll take care of the creature," she said, her eyes flashing with determination. "You focus on breaking the curse, Emilia."

Nephthys' magic enveloped the creature, binding it with chains of light and shadow. Emilia took advantage of the distraction to focus on Ahmose, using the Chronosphere to create a temporal echo that resonated with his heartbeat.

As the echo grew stronger, Emilia could see the curse that had taken hold of Ahmose begin to weaken. She poured all her energy into the Chronosphere, using its power to amplify her own magic.

Slowly but surely, the curse began to break, its hold on Ahmose faltering as Emilia's magic washed over him. The creature, sensing its control slipping, let out a deafening roar and struggled against Nephthys' bindings.

Ani and Kiya took advantage of the distraction to strike the final blow, their weapons slicing through the creature's defences and banishing it back to the underworld.

As the creature disappeared, Ahmose collapsed to the ground, freed from the curse's control. Emilia rushed to his side, helping him to his feet as Nephthys released her magic.

Together, the four of them stood victorious, their bond and determination having saved the day. But as they caught their breath and tended to their wounds, Emilia knew that their adventure was far from over.

The curse may have been broken, but the consequences of its power still lingered. Emilia could feel the time stream trembling, threatening to unravel the very fabric of reality.

"We need to find a way to stabilize the time stream," Emilia said, her mind racing with the implications. "Or risk losing everything we've fought for."

And so, their quest continues, as they embark on a new journey to restore balance to the time stream and ensure the future of the world.

As they journeyed on, Emilia began to notice strange occurrences around her. Time seemed to be warping and bending, as if the very fabric of reality was unravelling.

"Guys, I think we have a problem," Emilia said, her voice laced with concern. "The time stream is destabilizing. We need to find a way to fix it, fast."

THE TIME KEEPER'S QUEST

Ani, Kiya, and Nephthys exchanged worried glances. They knew that Emilia's connection to the time stream made her sensitive to its fluctuations.

"What can we do?" Ani asked, his hand on the hilt of his sword.

Emilia thought for a moment. "We need to find a temporal anchor. Something that can stabilize the time stream and prevent further damage."

Nephthys nodded. "I think I know of a place that might have what we're looking for. Follow me."

She led them to a hidden chamber deep within the temple, where a glowing crystal orb sat atop a pedestal.

"This is a temporal anchor," Nephthys explained. "It can absorb and redirect temporal energy. But we need to activate it."

Emilia reached out, feeling the orb's energy coursing through her veins. "I think I can do that."

As she touched the orb, Emilia felt a surge of power flow through her. The time stream around her began to stabilize, its fluctuations slowing and then stopping.

The four of them breathed a collective sigh of relief. They had done it. They had saved the time stream.

But as they turned to leave, Emilia noticed something strange. A figure, shrouded in shadows, watching them from the corner of the chamber.

"Who's there?" Emilia called out, her hand on the Chronosphere.

The figure stepped forward, revealing a mysterious woman with piercing blue eyes.

"I am the Guardian of Time," she said, her voice low and mysterious. "And you, Emilia, are the chosen one. You have saved the time stream, but now you must face the consequences of your actions."

Chapter 19

Emilia felt a shiver run down her spine as the Guardian of Time approached her. She had never seen anyone like her before.

"What do you mean by 'consequences'?" Emilia asked, her hand still on the Chronosphere.

The Guardian smiled, her eyes glinting with a knowing light. "You have altered the time stream, Emilia. You have changed the course of history. And now, you must face the repercussions of your actions."

Emilia felt a surge of fear. She had never intended to cause any harm.

"What repercussions?" she asked, her voice barely above a whisper.

The Guardian's smile grew wider. "Come with me, Emilia. And you will see."

Emilia hesitated, unsure of what to do. But something about the Guardian's words resonated deep within her. She knew that she had to follow her.

As they journeyed through time and space, Emilia saw glimpses of a world she had never known existed. A world where her actions had created a ripple effect, changing the lives of countless individuals.

She saw a future where her friends were alive and well, but also a future where they were gone, erased from existence.

Emilia's mind reeled as she struggled to comprehend the magnitude of her actions. She had never intended to cause such chaos.

The Guardian's words echoed in her mind: "You have altered the time stream, Emilia. You have changed the course of history. And now, you must face the repercussions of your actions."

Emilia knew that she had to make things right. She had to find a way to restore the original timeline, no matter the cost.

But as she turned to the Guardian, she saw something that made her heart skip a beat. A figure, hidden in the shadows, watching her every move.

"Who are you?" Emilia demanded, her hand on the Chronosphere.

The figure stepped forward, revealing a mysterious man with piercing green eyes.

"I am the Timekeeper," he said, his voice low and menacing. "And you, Emilia, are a threat to the time stream. You must be eliminated."

Emilia's eyes narrowed as she gazed at the Timekeeper. She could sense the power emanating from him, a power that seemed to rival even the Chronosphere's.

"What do you mean, I'm a threat?" Emilia asked, her voice firm and steady.

The Timekeeper sneered. "You've meddled with the time stream, Emilia. You've altered events that were meant to unfold. You must be stopped before you cause any more damage."

Emilia's grip on the Chronosphere tightened. "I won't let you harm me or my friends. We've done nothing wrong."

The Timekeeper chuckled. "You're naive, Emilia. You think you're the only one who can manipulate time? I've been doing it for centuries. And I won't let some amateur like you ruin everything."

With a flick of his wrist, the Timekeeper sent a temporal wave crashing towards Emilia. She raised the Chronosphere, and a blast of energy shot out, deflecting the attack.

The two engaged in a fierce battle, their powers locked in a struggle that seemed to shake the very fabric of time itself.

As they fought, Emilia began to realize that the Timekeeper was no ordinary opponent. He seemed to have an intimate understanding of the time stream, using his knowledge to exploit her weaknesses.

But Emilia refused to back down. With every ounce of strength she possessed, she pushed back against the Timekeeper's attacks, determined to protect her friends and the time stream.

Just when it seemed like the battle was reaching its climax, a sudden burst of energy intervened, sending both Emilia and the Timekeeper flying across the room.

As they struggled to their feet, Emilia saw a figure standing in the doorway - a figure she had thought she'd never see again.

"Mother?" Emilia whispered, her eyes wide with shock.

Her mother smiled, a hint of sadness in her eyes. "I'm sorry, Emilia. I should have told you the truth long ago. But now, I'm here to help you. We have to stop the Timekeeper together."

Emilia's mind raced as she tried to process her mother's sudden appearance. She had so many questions, but before she could ask any of them, her mother turned to face the Timekeeper.

"You're a hard man to find," Emilia's mother said, her voice dripping with sarcasm. "I've been searching for you for centuries."

The Timekeeper snarled, his eyes flashing with anger. "You're a fool for coming here," he spat. "You'll never leave this place alive."

Emilia's mother smiled sweetly. "We'll see about that."

With a wave of her hand, she sent a blast of energy shooting towards the Timekeeper. He attempted to deflect it, but Emilia's mother was too powerful. The energy struck him with incredible force, sending him flying across the room.

Emilia watched in awe as her mother battled the Timekeeper. She had never seen her like this before - so powerful, so confident.

As the fight raged on, Emilia began to realize that her mother was holding back. She could have easily defeated the Timekeeper, but she was letting him live.

Why?

Emilia's question was answered when the Timekeeper suddenly spoke up. "You'll never win," he snarled. "The time stream is mine to control."

Emilia's mother smiled again. "Not if I have anything to say about it."

With a final burst of energy, she struck the Timekeeper down. Emilia felt a surge of relief as the battle ended.

But as she approached her mother, she saw something that made her heart skip a beat. A strange device was attached to her mother's wrist, pulsing with an otherworldly energy.

"Mother, what is that?" Emilia asked, her voice trembling.

Her mother looked down at the device, a hint of sadness in her eyes. "It's a time machine," she said. "And I'm afraid I've been using it to manipulate the time stream."

Emilia's eyes widened in shock. "What do you mean?" she asked, her voice barely above a whisper.

Her mother sighed. "I've been trying to fix the time stream, Emilia. I've been trying to prevent the catastrophic future that's coming."

Emilia's mind raced. "But why? Why would you do that?"

Her mother's eyes filled with tears. "Because, Emilia, I'm the one who caused it. I'm the one who made the mistake that led to the future being destroyed."

Emilia felt like she had been punched in the gut. She couldn't believe what she was hearing.

"But why didn't you tell me?" Emilia asked, her voice shaking with anger and hurt.

Her mother reached out and took Emilia's hand. "I was afraid, Emilia. I was afraid of losing you. I was afraid of what might happen if you knew the truth."

Emilia pulled her hand away. "You should have told me," she said, her voice cold. "You should have trusted me."

Her mother nodded. "You're right, Emilia. I'm so sorry. I was wrong to keep it from you."

Emilia took a deep breath and tried to process everything she had just learned. She was still trying to wrap her head around it all when her mother spoke up again.

"Emilia, I need your help," her mother said, her voice urgent. "I need your help to fix the time stream. Will you help me?"

Emilia hesitated. She wasn't sure if she could trust her mother again. But something in her mother's eyes made her nod. "Yes," Emilia said. "I'll help you."

Chapter 20

Emilia and her mother stood facing each other, the tension between them palpable. Emilia's mind was reeling with questions, but she knew she had to focus on the task at hand.

"Okay, let's do this," Emilia said, her voice firm. "But first, tell me everything. I want to know what really happened."

Her mother nodded, taking a deep breath. "It started centuries ago, Emilia. I was a scientist, studying the time stream. I wanted to understand it, to learn how to manipulate it."

Emilia's eyes narrowed. "And then what happened?"

Her mother hesitated. "I made a mistake, Emilia. I created a rift in the time stream. And through that rift, a dark energy began to seep in."

Emilia's eyes widened. "Dark energy? What do you mean?"

Her mother's face was grim. "It's a power that consumes everything in its path. And it's been growing stronger ever since."

Emilia felt a chill run down her spine. "And what does this have to do with me?"

Her mother's eyes locked onto hers. "You, Emilia, are the key to stopping it. You have a special gift, one that allows you to manipulate the time stream."

Emilia's mind raced. "But why me? Why do I have this gift?"

Her mother smiled sadly. "Because, Emilia, you are my daughter. And I passed on my gift to you."

Emilia's eyes widened in shock. "You mean...I'm the result of your experiment?"

Her mother nodded. "Yes, Emilia. You are the product of my mistake."

Emilia's mind was reeling with questions and emotions. She felt like her whole identity was being turned upside down.

"But why did you keep this from me?" Emilia asked, her voice shaking with anger and hurt.

Her mother sighed. "I was afraid, Emilia. I was afraid of what might happen if you knew the truth. I was afraid of losing you."

Emilia took a step back, feeling like she was living in a dream. "So, you lied to me my whole life?"

Her mother nodded. "I'm so sorry, Emilia. I was trying to protect you."

Emilia's eyes narrowed. "Protect me from what?"

Her mother hesitated. "From the truth. From the danger that comes with your gift."

Emilia's mind raced. "What danger?"

Her mother took a deep breath. "There are those who would seek to use your gift for their own gain. They would stop at nothing to control you."

Emilia's eyes widened. "Who? What are you talking about?"

Her mother's face was grim. "The Order of the Timekeepers. They've been searching for you, Emilia. And they'll stop at nothing to find you."

Emilia's heart raced. "What do I do?"

Her mother's eyes locked onto hers. "You must learn to control your gift, Emilia. You must learn to use it to protect yourself."

Emilia nodded, determination burning within her. "I will. I'll learn everything I can."

Her mother smiled, a hint of pride in her eyes. "I know you will, Emilia. You're strong and capable. And I'll be here to help you every step of the way."

Emilia's mother handed her a small, intricately carved box. "This contains a powerful tool that will help you master your gift. But be warned, Emilia, the Order will stop at nothing to get it."

Emilia took the box, feeling a surge of energy emanating from it. She opened it, revealing a beautiful, glowing crystal.

"What is this?" Emilia asked, mesmerized.

"That's a Timekeeper's Crystal," her mother replied. "It will amplify your powers and help you control the time stream."

Emilia's eyes widened as she felt the crystal's energy coursing through her veins. She knew that this was the key to unlocking her true potential.

"But how do I use it?" Emilia asked, eager to learn.

Her mother smiled. "That's the easy part. Just focus your mind and channel the crystal's energy. You'll see."

Emilia nodded, determination burning within her. She was ready to master her gift and take on the Order.

As she held the crystal, Emilia felt a strange sensation wash over her. The room began to blur and fade away, replaced by a vision of a ancient temple.

"Where am I?" Emilia asked, disoriented.

Her mother's voice echoed in her mind. "You're in the Temple of the Timekeepers. That's where you'll find the answers you seek."

Emilia's vision shifted, revealing a mysterious figure cloaked in shadows.

"Who are you?" Emilia demanded.

The figure stepped forward, revealing a woman with piercing green eyes.

"I am the Guardian of the Temple," she said. "And you, Emilia, are the chosen one."

Emilia's mind raced. "Chosen for what?"

The Guardian smiled. "To wield the power of the Timekeepers and save the time stream from destruction."

Emilia's heart raced. She knew that this was her destiny.

"The time stream is fragile, Emilia," the Guardian said, her voice serious. "It's been damaged by the Order's actions, and if we don't act fast, it could unravel completely."

Emilia felt a surge of determination. "I won't let that happen," she said. "I'll do whatever it takes to protect the time stream."

The Guardian nodded, a hint of a smile on her face. "I knew I could count on you, Emilia. Now, let's get started."

With that, the Guardian led Emilia on a journey through the Temple of the Timekeepers, teaching her how to harness her powers and control the time stream. Emilia learned how to create temporal loops, manipulate time waves, and even bend the fabric of reality.

As she trained, Emilia discovered that her abilities were far more extensive than she had ever imagined. She was a natural Timekeeper, and with the Guardian's guidance, she quickly mastered the skills she needed to take on the Order.

But as Emilia's powers grew stronger, so did the danger. The Order was getting closer, and Emilia knew that she couldn't hide forever.

"Guardian, I need to ask you something," Emilia said, her voice serious.

"Of course, Emilia. What is it?"

"What happens if I fail?" Emilia asked, her heart racing with fear.

The Guardian's expression turned grim. "If you fail, Emilia, the time stream will be destroyed. And with it, the entire universe."

Emilia felt a chill run down her spine. She knew that she couldn't let that happen. She had to succeed, no matter what.

Emilia steeled herself for the challenge ahead. She knew that she couldn't fail, not now that she had come so far.

"I won't let that happen," Emilia said, her voice firm. "I'll do whatever it takes to protect the time stream."

The Guardian nodded, a hint of a smile on her face. "I knew I could count on you, Emilia. Now, let's get ready for the final battle."

With that, the Guardian led Emilia to a hidden chamber deep within the Temple of the Timekeepers. Inside, Emilia found a suit of armour unlike any she had ever seen.

"This is the Timekeeper's Armour," the Guardian said, her voice filled with reverence. "It's been passed down through generations of Timekeepers, and now it's yours."

Emilia's eyes widened as she took in the armour's beauty. It was made of a shimmering metal that seemed almost otherworldly.

"Put it on," the Guardian said, her voice urgent. "We don't have much time."

Emilia nodded, and with the Guardian's help, she put on the armour. It fit perfectly, and Emilia felt a surge of power run through her veins.

"I'm ready," Emilia said, her voice firm.

The Guardian nodded, a hint of a smile on her face. "Then let's go save the time stream."

With that, Emilia and the Guardian set off towards the final battle, ready to face whatever lay ahead.

Chapter 21

Emilia and the Guardian arrived at the entrance of the Order's headquarters, a towering fortress built on a desolate planet. Emilia could feel the dark energy emanating from within, and she knew that this was it – the final battle.

"Are you ready, Emilia?" the Guardian asked, her voice firm.

Emilia nodded, her heart racing with anticipation. "Let's do this."

With a deep breath, Emilia and the Guardian charged into the fortress, their weapons at the ready. The interior was dark and foreboding, lit only by flickering torches that cast eerie shadows on the walls.

As they ventured deeper, Emilia encountered hordes of Order soldiers, their eyes glowing with an otherworldly energy. Emilia fought valiantly, her Timekeeper's Armour glowing with power as she took down enemy after enemy.

But despite her best efforts, Emilia soon found herself surrounded by the Order's elite warriors. She fought hard, but they seemed to be gaining the upper hand.

Just when all seemed lost, the Guardian appeared, her sword flashing in the dim light. Together, Emilia and the Guardian fought off the warriors, their bond growing stronger with every passing moment.

Finally, they reached the heart of the fortress: the throne room. And there, on the throne, sat the Order's leader – the mysterious figure known only as "The Time Reaver".

"Welcome, Emilia," The Time Reaver said, his voice dripping with malice. "I've been waiting for you."

Emilia drew her sword, ready for the final showdown. "Let's end this."

The Time Reaver sneered at Emilia, his eyes gleaming with contempt. "You're a foolish girl, Emilia. You think you can defeat me? I have the power of time itself on my side."

Emilia smiled, her confidence growing. "I've come too far to back down now. I'll stop you, no matter what it takes."

With a wave of his hand, The Time Reaver summoned a horde of temporal minions, their bodies twisting and contorting in ways that defied human physics. Emilia charged forward, her sword flashing in the dim light, but The Time Reaver was relentless, using his powers to manipulate time and space.

Emilia found herself facing multiple versions of The Time Reaver, each one attacking her from a different angle. She fought hard, but The Time Reaver seemed to always be one step ahead.

Just when Emilia thought she was gaining ground, The Time Reaver unleashed a devastating temporal blast, sending Emilia flying across the room. Emilia struggled to get back to her feet, but The Time Reaver was already closing in for the kill.

In a desperate bid to turn the tables, Emilia reached deep within herself and tapped into the power of the time stream. The room around her began to distort and writhe, time itself bending to her will.

The Time Reaver stumbled back, his eyes wide with shock, as Emilia unleashed a devastating temporal counterattack. The two enemies clashed, their powers locked in a struggle that seemed to shake the very foundations of reality.

And then, in an instant, it was over. Emilia stood victorious, The Time Reaver defeated and his dark powers banished from the time stream. Emilia had saved the universe, but at what cost?

As the dust settled, Emilia surveyed the damage. The throne room was in shambles, the walls cracked and broken. But Emilia's attention was focused on the figure before her.

The Time Reaver, once so full of arrogance and confidence, now lay defeated and helpless. Emilia felt a sense of satisfaction, knowing that she had stopped him and saved the time stream.

But as she approached him, Emilia saw something unexpected. The Time Reaver's eyes, once gleaming with malice, now shone with a hint of recognition.

"Emilia," he whispered, his voice weak. "I know you."

Emilia's curiosity was piqued. "What do you mean?" she asked.

The Time Reaver's gaze seemed to bore into her soul. "I am your father," he said.

Emilia's world went white. She felt like she had been punched in the gut. "No," she whispered. "That's not possible."

The Time Reaver's smile was weak. "I'm afraid it's true, Emilia. I am your father, and I've been trying to protect you all along."

Emilia's mind raced. She didn't know what to believe. Part of her wanted to deny it, to reject the idea that this monster was her father. But another part of her, a small voice deep inside, whispered that it might be true.

As Emilia struggled to come to terms with this revelation, the Guardian appeared at her side. "Emilia, we need to talk," she said.

Emilia nodded, still trying to process the news. She followed the Guardian out of the throne room, leaving The Time Reaver behind. But Emilia knew that this was far from over. She had a feeling that her whole world was about to change forever.

"Emilia, I know this is a lot to take in," the Guardian said, her voice soft and gentle. "But you need to know the truth. The Time Reaver is indeed your father, and he's been trying to protect you from those who would misuse your powers."

Emilia's mind raced as she tried to process this information. She had always known that her parents were dead, but now she was faced with the possibility that her father was alive and had been hiding in plain sight.

"But why did he try to kill me?" Emilia asked, her voice shaking with anger and confusion.

The Guardian sighed. "He was trying to prevent you from falling into the wrong hands. He knew that your powers would make you a target, and he wanted to keep you safe."

Emilia's eyes narrowed. "By trying to kill me?"

The Guardian nodded. "I know it sounds crazy, but he believed it was the only way to protect you. He's been watching you from afar, Emilia, and he's proud of the strong woman you've become."

Emilia's heart raced as she tried to process this information. She didn't know what to believe or who to trust. But one thing was certain - she needed answers.

"I want to talk to him," Emilia said, her voice firm.

The Guardian nodded. "I'll take you to him."

Emilia followed the Guardian back to the throne room, her heart pounding in her chest. She was ready to face her father and demand answers. But as she entered the room, she saw something that made her blood run cold.

The Time Reaver was gone.

Emilia's eyes scanned the room, but there was no sign of The Time Reaver. She felt a surge of anger and betrayal. "Where is he?" she demanded.

The Guardian shook her head. "I don't know. He vanished into thin air."

Emilia's mind raced. She had so many questions, and now it seemed like she would never get the answers. She turned to the Guardian, her eyes blazing with determination.

"I'll find him," Emilia said. "And I'll get the truth out of him."

The Guardian nodded. "I'll help you, Emilia. We'll search the time stream together."

Emilia nodded, a plan forming in her mind. She would find The Time Reaver, no matter what it took. And when she did, she would make him pay for his betrayal.

As Emilia and the Guardian set out on their quest, they were unaware of the dangers that lay ahead. The time stream was full of secrets and surprises, and Emilia was about to face the biggest challenge of her life.

Chapter 22

Emilia and the Guardian had been searching the time stream for what felt like an eternity. They had scoured every corner of the universe, following every lead, every hint, every rumour. And finally, after all this time, they had found him.

The Time Reaver stood before them, his eyes gleaming with a malevolent light. Emilia could feel the power of the time stream coursing through him, and she knew that this was it – the final confrontation.

"You're a hard woman to find," The Time Reaver said, his voice dripping with sarcasm.

Emilia drew her sword, its blade shining with a fierce determination. "You're a hard man to kill," she retorted.

The battle was fierce, the two enemies clashing in a spectacular display of power and skill. Emilia fought with every ounce of strength she had, but The Time Reaver was a formidable foe.

Just when it seemed like Emilia was gaining the upper hand, The Time Reaver unleashed a devastating temporal blast, sending Emilia flying across the room. Emilia struggled to get back to her feet, but The Time Reaver was already closing in for the kill.

And then, just as all seemed lost, the Guardian intervened, her sword flashing in the dim light. The Time Reaver stumbled back, momentarily stunned, and Emilia took advantage of the reprieve.

With a fierce cry, Emilia launched herself at The Time Reaver, their blades clashing in a final, decisive blow. The outcome was far from certain, but one thing was clear – only one of them would walk away from this fight alive.

Emilia's blade clashed with The Time Reaver's in a shower of sparks, the two enemies exchanging blow for blow. But Emilia had the upper hand now, her determination and skill fuelled by her quest for justice.

With a final, mighty swing, Emilia struck The Time Reaver down, his body crumbling to dust as the time stream rejected his existence.

The Guardian approached Emilia, a nod of respect on her face. "You did it, Emilia. You saved the time stream."

Emilia stood tall, her sword still trembling with the force of her final blow. "It's over," she said, a sense of closure washing over her.

The Guardian smiled. "Not quite yet. There's one more thing."

Emilia raised an eyebrow as the Guardian led her to a nearby console. With a few swift keystrokes, the Guardian activated a device that began to glow with a soft, blue light.

"This is a temporal anchor," the Guardian explained. "It will stabilize the time stream, preventing any further distortions."

Emilia watched in awe as the device hummed to life, its energy enveloping the time stream. Slowly but surely, the distortions began to fade, the time stream repairing itself.

And with that, Emilia's quest was truly over. She had saved the time stream, restored balance to the universe, and found closure.

The Guardian turned to Emilia with a warm smile. "You've earned your rest, Emilia. Your name will go down in history as the hero who saved the time stream."

Emilia smiled, feeling a sense of pride and accomplishment. "It was a team effort," she said, nodding to the Guardian.

Together, they walked away from the console, leaving the time stream to its newfound stability. Emilia knew that new adventures awaited her, but for now, she was content to bask in the glow of a job well done.

Epilogue

Years passed since Emilia's victory over The Time Reaver. The time stream flourished, and the universe prospered. Emilia's name became synonymous with bravery and heroism, inspiring generations to come.

Emilia herself continued to explore the mysteries of the time stream, using her knowledge to help those in need. She became a respected mentor and teacher, guiding young adventurers on their own journeys through time.

One day, Emilia received a visit from a young woman named Maya, who possessed a remarkable talent for time manipulation. Emilia saw a spark of herself in Maya and took the young woman under her wing.

As they walked through the temporal gardens, Emilia shared her wisdom and experience with Maya. "Remember, the time stream is a powerful force," Emilia said. "Use your gifts wisely, and always protect the timeline."

Maya nodded, her eyes shining with determination. "I will, Emilia. I promise to carry on your legacy."

Emilia smiled, knowing that the future was in good hands. And as she watched Maya disappear into the time stream, Emilia realized that her own journey had come full circle.

The story of Emilia, the Timekeeper, became a legend, inspiring countless others to defend the time stream and explore its wonders.

And though Emilia's adventures had ended, her legacy would live on forever, a testament to the power of courage and determination.

THE END

Dear Reader,

I just wanted to take a moment to express my heartfelt gratitude for taking the time to read my book. Your willingness to invest your precious time in my story means the world to me.

As an author, there's no greater joy than knowing that my words have resonated with someone, and that my story has become a part of your journey. Your engagement with my work is what makes all the long hours, doubts, and sacrifices worthwhile.

I hope that my book has transported you to new worlds, introduced you to memorable characters, and sparked emotions that linger long after the final page. I hope it has made you think, feel, and reflect on your own experiences.

Your support and enthusiasm are what fuel my creativity and drive me to continue crafting stories that inspire, entertain, and connect us all.

Thank you again for being a part of my literary journey. I'm honoured to have shared my work with you, and I look forward to connecting with you through future stories.

With sincere appreciation and gratitude,
Muvhango Mahooa

For reviews, feedback or enquiries, please get in contact with the author using any preferred methodology from below :

Contact number : 083 698 5348

Email address : Muvhangomahooa17@gmail.com

Milton Keynes UK
Ingram Content Group UK Ltd.
UKHW042002281024
450365UK00003B/96